The Death of a Beekeeper

Lars Gustafsson
The Death of a Beekeeper

TRANSLATED FROM THE SWEDISH
BY JANET K. SWAFFAR AND GUNTRAM H. WEBER,
WITH AN AFTERWORD BY JANET K. SWAFFAR

A New Directions Book

Originally published as *En biodlares dod* by P. A. Norstedt and Söners Förlag, Stockholm, in 1978. This English translation is published by arrangement with Carl Hanser Verlag, Munich.

Assistance for the translation of this volume was given by The Swedish Institute, Stockholm, whose support is gratefully acknowledged.

The epigraph in this book is from Lars Gustafsson's poetry collection *Varma rum och kalla,* Copyright © 1972 by Lars Gustafsson, published by Bonnier, Stockholm. The English translation is from *Warm Rooms and Cold,* Translation Copyright © 1975 by Yvonne Sandstroem, published by Copper Beach Press, Providence, R.I.

Manufactured in the United States of America
First published clothbound and as New Directions Paperbook 523 in 1981
Published simultaneously in Canada by George J. McLeod, Ltd., Toronto

Library of Congress Cataloging in Publication Data
Gustafsson, Lars, 1936-
  The death of a beekeeper.
  (A New Directions Book)
  Translation of: En biodlares død.
  I. Title.
PT9876.17.U8B5613   1981   839.7'374   81-11182
ISBN 0-8112-0809-5   AACR2
ISBN 0-8112-0810-9 (pbk.)

New Directions Books are published for James Laughlin
by New Directions Publishing Corporation,
80 Eighth Avenue, New York 10011

"Dogs! Hangmen's servants!
Royal torture masters!
Haven't you understood?
You there, heating tongs over a coal fire!
I'm actually a donkey!
With the heart of a donkey and the bray of a donkey!
I never give up!"

The Death of a Beekeeper

Prelude

Kind readers. Strange readers. We begin again. We never give up. It is early spring 1975, the story begins in the middle of the thaw. The location is North Väst-manland.

The former elementary school teacher of Väster Våla, his name is Lars Lennart Westin, but he was often called "Weasel," was retired early when the school was closed down, the local elementary school in Ennora on the northern shore of the lake. He earns his living doing all kinds of things, primarily selling the honey produced by his beekeeping, which from time to time has been quite extensive. Since his divorce he has been living in a hut on the peninsula on the same latitude as the villages Vretarna and Bodarna, but, of course, on the east side of the lake. He has a small garden, a potato patch, a dog. Sometimes relatives come and visit him. He has a telephone, a television set, and a subscription to the *Vestmanlands Läns Tidning*. Since obtaining his divorce he has had no notable relationships with women.

The "Weasel" is not particularly old. He was born on May 17, 1936. But he looks much older than forty already, spent, with sparse hair, thin. He wears one of those glasses with narrow steel rims which intensify the impression of leanness. His financial situation is extremely modest, but that is not his problem.

What follows now are the notes he left behind. Left behind: for in this spring of 1975 in the middle of the thaw he finds out that he will not live to see the fall. He has terminal cancer, which, after some time, much too late, has been located in the spleen, with large metastases in the surrounding tissue.

The voice which you are going to hear is his, not mine, and therefore at this point I take my leave of you.

Inventory of Sources

1. The Yellow Notebook

Found on the shelf over the sink, unlined, size 16 × 6 cm., 80 pages, of which 76 are full. Yellow cover with the legend: NATIONAL ASSOCIATION OF SWEDISH BEEKEEPERS.

Contains very personal and very impersonal notations. Among the latter are a series of monthly calculations of household expenses, comments and notes concerning the care of the hives. Expediency dictated that only a few indicative samples be used in this edited version.

Begun February 1970.

2. The Blue Notebook

Found on the top row of books in the bookshelf. Legal size, lined, blue cover with the imprint *Sjöberg's Books Västerås*. Contains 112 pages, of which 97 have been written on both sides.

Contains various pasted newpaper clippings, excerpts from Westin's readings, and his own stories.

Begun no earlier than summer 1964.

3. The Damaged Notebook

So-called telephone pad. The bottom half of the cover torn off. Imprint WHO [CALLED?]. Found next to the telephone on the counter across from the sink in the kitchen. Contains local telephone numbers, a very few long distance numbers, and a smaller number of notes referring to the course of the disease.

Begun no earlier than 1970.

1. The Letter

. . . wind rose, yes, a really warm wind was blowing. It was the end of August last year, the dog had taken off, he had just begun this running away business then, and I went looking for him around eleven o'clock in the evening. The sky was overcast, it was so dark that you couldn't see the treetops anymore, but you could hear the wind moving through them the whole time. It was always the same, continuously strong, strangely warm wind. I remember having experienced something similar before, but I can't recall precisely when.

When I came to the path to the Sundblads', which runs along the lake, smelled the scent of the water and heard the waves beating without seeing them in the darkness, I clearly felt a small frog hopping over my shoe.

Then I did something I am sure I hadn't done since the fifties. I bent down quickly and moved my cupped hands through the wet grass just in front of the spot where it had to be.

This old trick always worked. It hopped straight into my hands, and I could hold it captive in my right hand as if in a cage, it was that small.

For a moment it sat there as if paralyzed, and I put both hands together to make a larger cage.

There I stood now listening to the wind, a frog in my hands as if locked in a cage, and the same warm wind was continuously moving through the trees. A sour smell came from the swamps on the wooded shore. I clearly felt the frog trembling in my hands.

And then suddenly it peed right on my hand.

I believe that is an experience not many people have had.

The pee of a frog is ice-cold. I was so surprised that I opened my hands and let it hop away. Thus I stood there, deeply moved, above me the wind passing through the treetops, and my hand cold from the pee of a frog.

We begin again. We never give up.

(The Yellow Book I:1)

I found the dog at the Sundblads'. He had been there the whole afternoon, had been fed pancakes and water. The really embarrassing thing was: when I tried to take him with me he didn't want to come. He resisted, planting his paws firmly on the rag rug in the kitchen.

That was embarrassing. They could easily have gotten the impression that I treated the dog so badly that he didn't dare go home with me. But that simply isn't true.

It is something else, and I simply don't understand what it can be. It really seems as if the dog was frightened in some peculiar way, and, in fact, for the third time now within a few weeks. Yet I'm not treating him any differently now than I have been for the past eleven years. It may be that I'm a bit short-tempered sometimes, but certainly not to the point of frightening him. The dog knows me inside and out, he has known me since he was a pup.

There is only one reasonable explanation: the dog is gradually getting so old that certain subtle changes are taking place somehow in the olfactory perceptions stored in his brain. And hence he simply doesn't recognize me anymore.

On the one hand I think that he can hardly see at all, on the other hand his eyesight is not very important to him.

During the winter in the early sixties I once used a ski track in the hills of Lake Märrsjön. At that time I was still the teacher at the old elementary school in Ennora, before it was moved to Fagersta, and could only go skiing on Saturdays and Sundays. It was a beautiful Sunday in February, a whole lot of people were using the track, and as I came over the crest of a hill I saw a man in a blue hooded jacket only thirty meters ahead of me.

The whole time the dog had been running several meters ahead of me, and he certainly knew that this man was there, he had been registered for several kilometers as a scent profile, as a smell in the smell center of the dog brain.

At this point the man, who is somewhat older, moves to the side to adjust something or maybe only to let me get by since I'm so close behind him.

Confound it, if the dog doesn't run right into him so that the man almost sat down on his behind right in the middle of the track!

For the dog a man dressed in blue doesn't exist, there is only an interesting smell which he follows and which gets stronger and stronger, and he relies on it so blindly that he doesn't even raise his head when he just about runs into the man.

It is definitely connected with the sense of smell. And nothing can be done about it. He has always been a good dog. And I hope he'll hold on for a long time yet.

I don't know what got into him. It really seems as if the dog doesn't recognize me anymore. Or more precisely: he recognizes me, but only from very close up, when I can bring him to really *see* me and *listen to* me instead of going only by the smell.

There is another explanation, of course, but it is so crazy that I can't believe it.

That all of a sudden I have taken on a different smell in some damnably subtle fashion which only the dog can perceive.

(The Yellow Book I:2)

Last fall quite a bit needed to be done to the beehives, new wood lining, new apertures on some of them, repairs on the frames, insulation material, but for some inexplicable reason I could never make myself do it. I don't quite understand why this is so. For some reason unclear to me I must have been very lethargic and passive last fall. Thank heavens the winter now, at the end of January, promises to be unusually warm. It is raining every day, and I stay in bed a little longer than usual in the winter darkness simply because it is pleasant to hear the rain falling on the roof.

But what if, in February, it gets cold again over night? What the devil shall I do then? The wooden cover of the hives is soaked with water, the tar paper on the roofs is damaged in many places. They will simply freeze to death. As punishment for my laziness last fall I am going to lose three, four hives.

Financially that would not make any difference since I finally got the lodging allowance raised by the municipality, but then living beings will die, and somehow that hurts.

A peculiar thing I discussed last week on the telephone with Isacsson over in Ramnäs: When a bee population dies, it is virtually as if an animal had died. One misses a personality, almost the way it is with a dog or, at very least, with a cat.

People are completely indifferent to a dead bee; they simply sweep it away.

The peculiar thing is that bees have precisely the same attitude. There is virtually no other animal species which has such a total lack of interest in the death of their kind.

11

If I squash a few bees by carelessly replacing a frame, the others drag them off as if they were dealing with some broken machines. But first they always get the pollen, if there happens to be any.

What now if they experience it in the same way? That it is the swarm that represents the individuality, the intelligence.

There are populations with enormous personality. There are lazy and hard-working, aggressive and gentle bee populations. There are even flighty and unreliable ones, and heaven knows whether there are populations with a sense of humor and others without it.

For example the swarming fever! That is precisely the way it is with a nervous, temperamental, impatient human being. A poor lover; no patience.

And the single bee just as impersonal as a cog in a clockwork.

(The Yellow Book I:3)

In August, when the children were here, they wanted to play badminton with me. For children of divorced parents I think they really had a very pleasant summer vacation. After all, they were here several times. In June and in August.

It was on that particular occasion, at any rate, while we were playing badminton, that it felt *just that way.*

But at that time I was absolutely certain that it was lumbago and forgot all about it. I naturally thought that I had pulled a muscle in my back. I had to quit playing immediately.

But is there a kind of lumbago that hurts so damned much that you taste blood?

(The Yellow Book I:4)

Are Swedes more patient than other nationalities? That is something I don't know much about. During my lifetime I haven't gotten around to much traveling. Two bicycle trips through Denmark at the beginning of the fifties, a ping-pong tournament in Kiel, and several backpacking trips over the border to Norway, way up north near Lake Femund through Orsa and Idre, that isn't much really. I tend to look at the world outside of Sweden as a literary phenomenon, something that exists in books and magazines.

Large distances frighten me. Paris is something which lives in the Goncourt brothers' diaries, the most modern London is that of the early novels of Aldous Huxley.

If I really went to these places I presumably wouldn't be able to get my bearings. I would find them irrelevant. I just read in the local paper that they now have sky-scrapers in Paris.

In my system, different times operate in different places. In Paris, for example, the mortar dust of the commune has hardly settled. What kind of a time operates here? The now.

So, are the Swedes more patient than other nationalities? The day before yesterday the waiting room of the X-ray ward in the Västerås district hospital. Pungent odor of woolen clothing, wet wool clothing. Everything full of people, on chairs, on benches, everywhere. A boy with terrible bruises covering the right side of his face. He had had an accident on a moped the evening before and was in pain. An old man from Kolbäck, who had come on the morning bus. He very much hoped that he would be able to catch the last bus of the evening. "They take their time around here." This was his second visit within a week. Everyone had a numbered ticket in their hand. The mysteries of waiting in line: sometimes the nurse calls in two or three patients at once, sometimes only one. Sometimes everything comes to a halt for an hour at a time. And the way everyone *looks up* every time the nurse appears.

Like a mechanical *Glockenspiel* whose figures move once on the hour; a door opens, someone comes out, someone goes in. A stinking drunk fellow with lots of bandaids on his forehead, under his eyes, on his chin, is brought in by two policemen. He gets treated right away.

Most of the sixty or seventy people in the room are in a greater or lesser degree of pain. With some of them you can tell by the way they sit, by the way they get up and pace restlessly back and forth.

But hardly anyone talks about it, they don't even say that something is hurting them (and this "hurting" can mean anything on a scale ranging from minor complaints to stabbing pains). Instead they talk about poor bus connections, about rail buses, about visits and return visits. It appears as if some of them live only to go to the hospital now and then. They actually feel fairly comfortable there. Their sickness gives them an identity. That goes for some of the oldest and least demanding.

Because of their sickness they arouse an interest which no one had in them when they were healthy.

Something about their patience irritates me terribly, makes me aggressive. They shouldn't settle for that . . . For what? For waiting so long to be X-rayed, for the strangely impersonal, assembly-line treatment, where

15

nobody cares that they sit there the whole day after waiting so early in the morning at their wintery bus stops, that they sit there waiting to be next, unable to get a bite to eat for fear of losing their place on the waiting list?

And in spite of everything, always a kind of camaraderie, always somebody who is ready to sound the alarm if the nurse should call out your name while you happen to be in the rest room for a cigarette. Or do I think that it is the pain itself that they should protest, that they should not accept? Proletarians of pain, unite!

(The Yellow Book I:5)

WHAT DOESN'T DESTROY ME, MAKES ME STRONGER. (Friedrich Nietzsche, German philosopher, 1844–1900)

(The Yellow Book I:6)

February 1975   *Swedish Crowns*

Grocer   —375:40
Sugar   —42:90
Tobacco   —32:50
Nails and misc. hardware   —16:00
Doctor   —7:00
Oil and gas   —75:00 (approx.)

Total expenditures   —548:80

National Assoc. of Beekeepers, bonus   + 16.—
Grocer, honey   +255.—
Health insurance   +304.—
repaired Sundblad's pump motor   + 50.—

Gross income in February   +625.—
Net   76.—

(The Yellow Book I:7)

18

When the letter from the district hospital in Västerås finally came, I didn't want to open it, so I laid it aside, leafed through newspapers and magazines, looked at a few bills and decided that I would not be able to pay them until next month anyway, and ended up taking the dog for a good long walk.

It was gray, pleasant February weather, fairly cold and hence not too damp, and the whole landscape looked like a pencil sketch. I don't know why I like it so much. It is pretty barren and yet I never get tired of moving about in it. I have spent a fairly considerable portion of my life here.

As long as I was married, I lived in Trummelsberg and drove the car to the schools; there were quite a few transfers over the years. Since I was trained as an elementary school teacher as well as a vocational teacher I could pretty much pick and choose my work during the last few years, as one school consolidation followed the other. And I became more and more a vocational teacher. The classes in elementary school were getting too large, I felt, and besides, I had better working hours that way.

Then, after I obtained my divorce, I moved here, moved deeper into the landscape, so to speak, and at the same time I gave up my teaching profession. There wasn't any money left over anyway after support payments, and so I simply gave up earning money, and instead I got thirty bee colonies.

Much to my astonishment, that worked just as well. Crises occur only when I have to go somewhere, like now when I have to go to the hospital.

19

When the letter from the district hospital finally came I simply put it aside and took a walk. I felt very calm and observed very thoroughly all of the bare hardwood trees along the way. I am really in love with these bare branches in front of a lead-colored sky. It is as if they were letters of a strange language, trying to tell me something.

The whole neighborhood with its boarded-up summer houses, snow-covered gardens, boats on racks, is now somehow incomparably more beautiful than in summer. Then the place is swarming with people. I have gotten to know quite a few of them over the years, some even invite me to visit for a game of cards or a little glass of something on the veranda, and that is a pleasant feeling. I am by no means an unsociable person. But here, this is real life. Whether good or bad, whether lonely or beautiful, it is my real life. And now something stronger than I, stronger than all the courts and governments and agencies, is trying to take it away from me.

It's not fair.

After I had walked around the entire peninsula and in doing so, by the way, had disturbed a moose family which was sniffing around behind the barn in Bruslings meadow, I came to the following conclusions:

Either this letter says that it's nothing bad. Or it says that I have cancer and am going to die. And naturally there is a high probability that it says that I do.

The smartest thing for me would be not to open it, because if I don't open it, there is still going to be some kind of hope.

And this hope will give me some latitude. Only a little

bit, to be sure, because it won't stop the pain, but it will be a very general pain, it won't remind me of anything in particular, I will be able to integrate it into my life, why shouldn't I be able to do that? I have been able to accept so many other things.

When the letter finally arrived, I took the dog for a walk around the entire peninsula, and when I came back I had made a decision: I will never open it.

It stood next to the table-setting on the flowered table-cloth in the kitchen, outside the birds were pecking on their board just like always, there had been even more thaw in the meantime, it was actually dripping already from the gutters. A brown envelope with a window, in the upper left-hand corner: District Hospital, Västerås, Central Laboratory. I felt the letter. There was only one sheet of paper, apparently folded in the middle. I held it up to the window. One couldn't see through.

If I open it, I thought, how is it going to change me? If it says that I only have a few months to live, am I going to be petrified? Paralyzed? Will I have to go to some hospital? Probably. And spend the last months in a bed with the pain getting stronger and stronger while I get thinner and weaker and am no longer in control of my own situation.

But if I open it now and it says the laboratory tests have shown that the samples they removed are from benign growths? That it is a stomach ulcer or a gallstone and must be treated with an operation and an appropriate diet and that it is extremely dangerous to run around with a gallstone and not be treated by a doctor?

21

What if I just get worse and worse in the event that I don't open this letter? Perhaps in time a new letter will come, but by then it will probably be much too late.

When the letter came I didn't open it but first went for a long walk with the dog.

When I came back home, I had begun to play with the idea of not opening it at all.

Somehow I played a little too long with this idea, only a tenth of a second too long, but that sufficed.

If this letter contains my death, then I refuse it.

One shouldn't get involved with death. I had the good fortune of learning that fairly early, it is a rule which has stood me in good stead throughout my whole life.

According to Wilhelm Wundt, who in his day had a not inconsiderable reputation as a psychologist, as I gather from the *Nordic Conversational Encyclopedia,* there are three kinds of pain. There are dull pains, stabbing pains, and burning pains.

In contrast to the terms for color perception, language has not developed any special words to define these various sensations. They don't have names of their own.

Perhaps that is because two people can see the same colors while two people can't possibly experience the same pain?

Mine is dull. Not exclusively. On some days it burns, too, but most of the time it's dull.

I believe it really began during that night when the dog had run away, because deep in my sleep I felt, for the first time, this strange, dull tension in the kidney area, as if someone were pumping up a soccer ball which he had

22

smuggled in there, pulsing, slowly, without the least concern whether I move or not.

At any rate I noticed it for the first time during the night when the dog had run away.

Most of the time it starts at night. I dream of it long before it has awoken me, it exists as something threatening in my dream, and I am constantly trying to *turn away* from it, not to look at it, I literally turn my head away from it in the dream, and in spite of this it keeps coming closer and forces me to *look at it* and awakens me.

Up until Christmas the pills helped pretty much—I first got them in Fagersta, when they still thought it was a kidney stone. (Right at the beginning, by the way, I thought it was lumbago, and later that it was the prostate, but as it turned out, I didn't have the slightest notion where it hurts when you have a prostate infection.)

Now, just a short time after Christmas, it's clear that the fairly strong pills for kidney stones—thank God they keep renewing my prescription—can no longer alleviate it. Not that the pain has gotten stronger, but rather the pills, e.g., my nervous system, have somehow lost their grip on it.

It has given me a body again; not since puberty have I had such a strong awareness of my body. I am intensely present in it.

Only: this body is the wrong one. It's a body with burning coals in it.

And then of course the hopes. Last week I was virtually certain for several days that it would slowly disappear, everything was as usual, I had almost forgotten how normal my body could be before the pain back there

23

really started. Of course I hardly dared to hope, but hoped anyway.

I took little walks and noticed that in the last months the pain had actually colored the landscape in a peculiar way. Here and there is a tree where it really hurt, here and there is a fence against whose post I struck my hand in passing. When I returned home during these pain-free days, the pain was, so to speak, caught hanging on the fence.

Pain is a landscape.

Then, of course, it came back, on Saturday evening, not all at once, but slowly, in tiny spurts, somewhat like a dog following a scent.

It took quite a few visits to the doctor before they asked themselves whether it could possibly be cancer. And then quite a number of additional visits to the doctor and many days in waiting rooms with this proletariat of pain, until they decided to take all kinds of tissue samples and blood samples to make a comparative study. It took quite a while to get all the samples. It got to be November, it got to be December.

Then I didn't hear a thing from them until yesterday, that is, the last day of February.

When the letter finally came, I didn't open it right away. Instead, I took a long walk with the dog and thought about the situation. The landscape was unchanged, very gray, naked trees with touching pencil twigs. On the lake, thick ice with wet snow on top of it, now at last, in February.

24

I sat there for some time and stared at the letter, feeling how thick and heavy it was, until it got much too cold in the kitchen because the kitchen stove went out for lack of wood. When I finally looked up, it was getting dark outside. It was already late afternoon, a typical February afternoon when dusk starts as early as four o'clock.

Finally I went out after all, got wood, and relit the fire. I used the letter to light it.

(The Yellow Book I:8)

2. A Marriage

. . . concerning this topic, by the way, a quite peculiar story of a meeting comes to mind. Not far from here there is a young lady, almost a girl still, who is very pretty and has a good figure. I had never seen her from a distance of less than fifty meters and found her quite attractive. Her face had strikingly vivid color, and her large eyes were very dark, her neck long and white. For a long time I had been tempted by a delicious urge to fall in love with her; but I never saw her anywhere but at the organ concerts at the church in Väster Våla. In the first years after my divorce, my contact with people, aside from my work, was extremely limited.

Then, finally, I really wanted to see whether what I imagined about her was true and found myself a good opportunity. At a concert of the Köping Quartet, during intermission, I went up to her in the vestibule of the church and greeted her.

I had no other plan, no other intention, than simply to hear what she would say. So I addressed her in a casual, courteous manner, but at the very moment I was about to open my mouth in order to introduce myself to her and, in so doing, got my first really good look at her, I would have preferred to remain silent.

I saw a large number of disgusting little pimples and pustules on her face, as if she had some peculiar type of skin disease, and that made me change my intentions immediately. However, I continued the conversation and her response was relaxed, in a very congenial and polite way. To tell the truth: it is not out of the question that I happened to make her acquaintance on one of those burdensome and awkward days when sex is self-prohibitive; around here she is really considered a beauty.

29

In spite of everything, I felt somehow relieved after this meeting. It freed me of something which seemed like the not altogether pleasant overture to a disruption of tranquility. And which perhaps had something to do with my bad habit of fixating on all possible objects which attract my restless attention.

. . .

But one must ask oneself after all: when we love someone, or perhaps better said, fall in love with someone, what are we really falling in love with?

Do we love our image of a person, or do we love that individual in his or her own right?

Perhaps we can only relate to our own imaginings? Perhaps we are only in love with our own images?

. . .

Love and geographical distance. When a person we love goes away on the train, we sometimes very clearly experience a kind of relief. We are escaping reality and can complacently return to living with an image.

What is the maximum distance from which you can love a person? A girl whom I loved very dearly in my school days, her name was Monica, emigrated to California. We exchanged letters for many years, but then, predictably, the whole thing petered out.

Did she exist at that time (for me)? Or had the person I related to been reduced to an image long before that?

What is the maximum distance from which you can love a human being? 1,000 kilometers? 25 kilometers? It has been an old wish of mine to have a lover in Skultuna. That is a truly wonderful distance, you travel precisely one half-hour to get there. In the summer perhaps a little quicker, when it's icy, on the other hand, it will go a bit slower.

What is the maximum distance from which you can love a human being?

Answer: less than a millimeter. And without a name.

. . .

When we had finally decided to get a divorce and Margaret was already thinking about finding an apartment in Västerås, something very peculiar happened. We went around in our apartment, looked at various things, and determined which books were hers, which mine, where she had purchased this or that, whether she should take this old file cabinet.

We both got into a really good mood, were almost exhilarated. We teased and talked with one another in a way that we hadn't done in over two years, somehow we were both relieved and astonished how real each of us appeared to the other.

We didn't have to live with images anymore.

(The Blue Book I:1)

. . . February of 1968 or 1969, I had been elected—to this very day I have no idea why—vice-chairman of the Swedish Field Biologists' Association. We had held our annual convention in the Medborgarhuset in South Stockholm, and as I stepped out into the February evening, it must have been around six o'clock, it was already completely dark. I was staying at the Malmen Hotel on the opposite side of the street, but since I was rather at loose ends, I decided to take a walk although it was only fourteen degrees above zero.

I went down the Folkungagatan; there was hardly anybody about, it was Sunday evening, the new moon stood in the sky, a thin layer of snow covered even the automobile tracks.

I went down to the harbor and then up the Stigbergs-gatan, on the way to Sista Styfverns Trappa, through virtually forgotten parts of town which have not changed in the least since the days of August Strindberg, a peculiar, cold city in the northern reaches of Scandinavia, little red framehouses on the mountainside, wooden steps, houses with the smell of tar, names reminiscent of the Baltic Sea, of Estonians and Finns, a city in a city, which looks exactly like the little towns of my home province and is just as defenseless as they are, a city in which everything has been imposed from above, regulations, taxes, inductions into armies which froze in Slavic swamps, even the bourgeois revolution was imposed from above.

I was somewhat exhausted after spending the whole day in a smoke-filled, poorly ventilated room in the Medborgarhuset, there had been some fairly strenuous

32

debates about the field biologists' budget, and besides that I was preoccupied with another matter which I don't want to discuss here.

As I emerge, I have no other thought in my head than that of going down the Folkungagatan. I walk mechanically, my sheepskin cap pulled down over my ears. For blocks, without actually thinking of anything in particular.

As I get to the warehouses at the Stadsgården, I am suddenly aware that I have been thinking about something after all: *about my childhood in Stockholm.*

It is winter, sometime around 1880, very cold, a lot of snow. We live in the small framehouses down by the Carlberg canal, which is completely frozen over, and in the afternoons, after school, we children skate on the frozen canal, with these old-fashioned skates whose tips curve upward like pokers. All that is very vivid. My little sister has difficulty tying the skates to her clumsy high-buttoned boots, and I help her with the laces. We glide through the dull, diffused light between afternoon and evening. Large barges, smelling of tar, are frozen solid into the ice, we go on board and look around, although that is forbidden. We find several beer bottles left by the stevedores on the deck, the really old-fashioned green kind with long necks.

And one afternoon in the bushes along the canal I discover the frozen corpse of a young woman, only an arm protrudes out of the ice, it is a young woman who drowned herself in the canal some time last fall and now her body is frozen solid in the ice. It isn't frightening at all, it is almost natural that a young woman is frozen

33

solid into the ice, it's only very sad, and I feel very sorry for her.

When I get home, however, and report my discovery, there is great excitement, people run out, ice cutters come from the city with their long saws, we children are not allowed to watch . . .

When I get to this point, I look up and it goes right through me: GOOD GOD, I NEVER HAD A CHILD-HOOD IN STOCKHOLM. And certainly not around 1880!

A gullible person would, at this point, start talking about transmigration of the soul and about memories of a previous existence. But, of course, such complicated explanations are not at all necessary.

When the unconscious is left to its own devices for a while, it simply begins to make things up. It creates an identity for itself, adjusts to its surroundings, produces, quite spontaneously, new forms to fill in the sudden vacuum which is created when we forget our everyday reality.

Apparently the unconscious mind does not fear anything quite so much as the sensation *of not being anyone at all.*

This zealous rascal was already at work compiling a new biography for me!

(The Blue Book II:4)

People who are going to be important to us we meet not just once, but at least twenty times before we begin to take the signs seriously.

At any rate that has always been my experience.

And we avoid them as long as we possibly can.

Margaret and I must have first met while attending the vocational school at Västerås. I attended the five-year program of the school, and she went into the four-year program. Most of the students in the four-year program were from the country; because it was so difficult and burdensome for them to go back and forth with buses and trains the whole school year, their parents naturally tried to keep the time their children spent at school to a minimum.

For that reason all the students who came from Surahammar and Hallstahammar, from Kolbäck, Rytterne, and Strömsholm to attend the high school in Västerås were, perhaps, somewhat more mature and independent than the rest of us who lived in the city, and they kept to themselves somewhat, formed their own clique.

From this time I recall her as being a thin, fairly quiet, small blonde girl, apparently never warm enough, since all winter she wore a pointed knit cap of a ridiculous cut, which came below her ears. You couldn't see she had blonde hair until well into spring.

She appeared to be quite shy.

At that time I was interested exclusively in another girl in her class, a tennis player with long dark hair, big eyes, prematurely developed breasts, and high cheekbones such as, strangely enough, the girls in Västmanland sometimes have. For the life of me I cannot remember her name. These two, Margaret and she, were friends, or at least they were seen together frequently, an unequal pair, the way it often is in such friendships where one is attractive and the other not at all.

I think she sometimes tried to talk with me, at least she maintained as much in the course of the ten years that I was married to her, but she says that I treated her as if she didn't exist.

When I think back, I get the terrible feeling that I simply found her just a wee bit repellent. She had a somewhat unpleasant emanation, or at least that was my reaction when I saw her.

Was this unpleasantness basically attractive? Or was it maybe a premonition that she would be enormously more important for me later on than she was at that time?

The only thing I can recall with precision from this period was a wild but totally suppressed hatred which I felt for the entire outside world: for the teachers, the school, even my peers, yes, for the entire outside world, since it appeared absolutely determined to treat me with all the hostility it could muster, to bring me to my knees, to discipline me, always claiming the rights of the stronger.

And this little, rather blonde, somehow helpless girl appeared to be as suppressed as I was, was presumably just as bitter as I was. Small wonder that I didn't find her particularly interesting! What I needed were well-adjusted people.

When I came to Uppsala and registered for the elementary school teachers' seminar, most of my fellow students had already been there for quite a while. I had been in the military for some time, had had noncommissioned officer's training with the navy, and by the time I got to the seminar everyone I knew from Västerås was already at the university.

Margaret came to the seminar a year later.

I saw her again at a dance. I don't believe that I intended to ask her to dance, but for some reason I did anyway. And thus I discovered the peculiar sensual warmth she radiated. I danced very close.

But only once.

After that I went home with a completely different girl, about whom, by the way, I only recall that she was much taller than I, and I believe I even slept with her.

Sleeping with Margaret somehow would have seemed *banal* to me.

During my studies in Uppsala I bummed around quite a bit. The teachers' seminar was really not very demanding, I had my only serious difficulties learning to play the organ, those damned pedals weren't inclined to mind me very well, and when I learned to drive a car some ten years later, the driving instructor complained that I treated the pedals of the automobile as though they were organ pedals. Aside from the pedals, the seminar in Uppsala was mere childishness, child's play or whatever one says, and I spent most of my time running after girls.

I don't know why, I assume it was a kind of restlessness, but I was interested in seduction.

A somewhat too exalted turn of phrase, certainly . . . but seduction was precisely what mattered to me.

I wanted to prove that I was *real*. And one can prove

37

that in only one way: by having an impact on another human being. The stronger the impact, the stronger one's sense of having proven one's own reality.

In those years I had a great need to be seen. And when one succeeds in seducing someone, one also succeeds in being seen.

Back then there were fabulous dances in Uppsala, especially the Wednesday parties of the Västmanland-Dalarna House were fantastic; a mad throng, the scent of cheap perfume, the girls on one side of the dance hall and the boys on the other. It was a miracle that the heat didn't melt the lacquer on the portraits of the former honorary chairmen who hung there in full regalia.

One only needed to take one's pick. In a peculiarly impersonal way.

For me, however, the somewhat shy, somewhat reserved girls were the most interesting; those who could be changed in one way or another.

The girls who trembled a little when one danced with them. Whose bodies tensed a little somehow.

I believe I took it all pretty mechanically. I mean: I set a chain of events in motion, and this chain of events served exclusively to prove something to me about myself.

("Myself"—"I myself": nowadays I find this expression somewhat stupid. It simply lacks all meaning.

I can't precisely explain, however, what I mean.)

At that time I had terribly little money. Money was worth more than it is today, but on the other hand one also had to make do for a much longer period of time with the student loans which one received, and if one didn't finish the requirements in time, one was really in bad shape.

In the beginning there were three of us, Bertil, Lennart, and I, we had rented two large rooms in the Svartbäkken Quarter. But after one semester Bertil and Lennart began to withdraw.

After all, they both went to the university and gradually found their own circle of friends. But I suppose that wasn't the only reason. Since both of them were hard-working—Bertil died a few years later, but that's a different story—since both were hard-working and ambitious, they felt I lured them into the bars too often, and none of us could really afford that.

I remember that until the latter part of November we went coatless into the bars in order to save the few kronen you usually had to pay the cloakroom attendants.

Acquaintances who saw me again some fifteen years later would tell me that I had changed a great deal, that I had really calmed down.

I never quite understood what they meant by that. For my part, I never had the sense of changing.

But apparently I was considered fairly unreliable and a bit of a rake at that time. I even think there were people who made up wild stories about me.

What I remember best is the eternal problem with money, the whole misery of constant borrowing here and there; debts which one had to pay back and debts which one could conceivably disregard, and this unpleasant air of rejection that people assumed toward one who had borrowed money once too often without paying it back.

Toward the end, the last year, it was worst of all. It was a chaotic year. To the present day it is a mystery to me how I could possibly have gotten through my final examinations as well as I did.

At that time I was friends for a while with a girl named Kerstin. It must have been the spring of 1958. I still think that she was genuinely fond of me, almost loved me, or at least there was something about me which must have fascinated her. But at the same time I think I have never known a human being who was so obviously afraid of me.

Afraid of what? God knows!

Much later I thought about it and pieced together all kinds of subtle explanations, I read her letters and saw her girlishly sensitive analyses of my soul (egotist, egocentric, unable to have a relationship with another human being, etc.), but eventually I came to a completely different conclusion: the reasons had to be social ones.

She came from a quite nice physician's family in Lidingö, not one of the tremendously successful ones, but all the same a very "cultivated" parental home, and studied for a Master of Philosophy in literary history and Nordic languages.

It was very clear that I could not offer her any kind of future.

She found me attractive, but from the social point of view I was a pretty dubious character.

I believe other people regarded me as more of a failure than I did.

One Sunday morning when I woke up at her place, we

got into an argument, I don't remember anymore what it was about, it was a brilliant Sunday morning. The apartment was in the Östra Ågatan, across from the castle, and this castle always had a unique beauty in the morning light. I went to the apartment door to get the *Dagens Nyheter,* Sunday mornings it usually came through the mail slot at this hour, it was, by the way, just that time in spring when the newspapers began to advertise bathing suits; I remember that because I noted ads for bathing suits all over the paper while I walked back, but then we continued this argument, and she said something, I can't for the life of me remember what it was, but it prompted me to get up and leave.

That is a terrible story. I think a part of my life ended with it.

(The remaining portion is approaching its end this winter.)

I was very desperate.

Three weeks later, several days before the end of April, I ran into Margaret. I hadn't seen her for a long time . . .

(The Yellow Book II:1)

Sudden thaw, a long walk with the dog, the pain well under control in the last few days, mainly toward four or five o'clock in the morning, but not so bad that I can't fall asleep again.

I must have been a bit distracted for several days, because in the meantime the entire landscape has changed. A moist fog everywhere, along the path there is a strong smell of earth and decaying birch trunks, and incomprehensibly a flock of crows, with really big crows, which otherwise like to stay down by the railroad viaduct on country road 251, have come here to the edge of the woods. They sit down there in the trees next to the fence, and all morning long I hear their raucous voices. It is also getting light somewhat earlier already. I wonder what summer will be like this year? Wet and cool like the last one or perhaps one of those very hot ones?

I also wonder frequently whether I will be allowed to find out. In any case the boat must get a good caulking. Last fall it leaked in the stern like a sieve. It was tied up at the boat dock for a ridiculously long time, hammering against it right up to the beginning of the fall storms. At that time I still felt pretty good, but apparently I was not particularly enterprising last fall.

. . . I thought again about Margaret. In this fog or in this springlike vapor, as one might perhaps say, I miss her again somehow. Her careful steps on the rug early in the morning—she always got up first and made coffee—her habit of laying the newspaper in very orderly and careful fashion on the newspaper pile in the cupboard under the sink before I had an opportunity to read it, her almost unbearable habit of beginning to work about ten or ten-thirty at night. It is such things which one remembers.

42

And now, especially when the pains begin, I miss her very much.

At the same time it is very clear that the whole affair was utterly impossible. It is a sheer wonder that it lasted as long as it did.

Everything, our whole life together, was based on one very simple principle, on one agreement:

Looking at one another was forbidden. I mean, really looking at one another.

It is a quite complicated game to maintain such an agreement for a period of twelve or thirteen years and not even let the mask fall when one is furious or very unhappy; as if one were locked up with someone for a long time in a very small room under the condition that one's back be perpetually turned on the other.

Naturally one has to ask oneself what is behind such an agreement.

I believe it is pain. A kind of primeval pain which one carries around with one from childhood on and which one dare not reveal at any price. Much more important than the presence of the pain is keeping it hidden.

But why was it so important then to hide it?

Sometimes we worked at the same school, sometimes at different ones. It went best when we saw each other during the day, too. When one was gone the whole day and we saw each other for the first time in the evening, there would always be a critical moment. This always happened some time after dinner, when the first report of the day's events was concluded, shortly after coffee, right before the television newscast, there was a kind of ebb tide, the water withdrew, the rocks became visible.

(The Blue Book II:2)

She was fairly small, always moved lightly, almost skipping, and spoke with a pleasant, soft voice. She had a lovely, a very stimulating curiosity about people, about the world, she read many books, it was fun to talk with her. She was seriously interested in almost everything that crossed her path, except perhaps in me.

That last spring in Uppsala had already become early summer. There were not very many people in the city anymore, I had stayed there because I had gotten a job as a Swedish teacher for foreign students and had moved into the center of the city into a room in Bäverns Gränd, which a friend who was traveling over the summer was letting me use.

She came with some girlfriend and sat down on the terrace of this small café, right next to the cathedral, which usually puts out a few tables, its name I believe was Cathedral Cellar. I can still remember the headlines on the newspaper placards in the little tobacco shop across the way, they dealt with a new, complicated phase in the ongoing argument about pension reform which, at that time, at the close of the fifties, was raging strongest. I remember that so particularly because I kept looking at the headlines while we were speaking with one another.

Her friend was a thin, angular little girl, very narrow face, glasses.

A copy of Margaret, one could say. She didn't say much, but I remember that I was continually comparing the two, as if this comparison were somehow important. And without knowing precisely what I really wanted to achieve in doing so.

Everything appeared clear from the outset, as if it had

44

been arranged for years. We sat there and talked with one another, by the way, about this part of the country here, sat there and recognized ourselves in each other. There was no place, no lake, no steelworks ruins, no discontinued old railway line in this neighborhood which she did not know. She had spent her summer vacation in northern Västmanland since she was a little girl.

I sat there in the light of the summer evening, and recognized the landscape through her.

I believe that's the way it started.

She has always been what one calls a really lovely girl, there was nothing to complain about in her appearance. (Her eyes have become more and more interesting with the years.)

For that reason it is utterly incomprehensible to me why I was always a little embarrassed and felt myself exposed when I was going somewhere with her in the street and met an acquaintance. Was it simply the fact that we revealed our relationship which embarrassed me?

(The Yellow Book II:2)

It was a rather quiet life. For years it was truly quiet, nothing more, nothing less, and very idyllic. We lived here and there in Västmanland, were employed by various schools as teachers, decorated the old apartments that came with the job until they became really livable, with Margaret's handwoven rugs and my cabinets and all the things that I had built, largely on my own, in various vocational shops.

Maybe we moved a bit too frequently, and we always stayed out in the country—that was something like a lifestyle; we, after all, both had some kind of (very vague) attitude of protest against the society around us. A protest of vegetable gardeners, so to speak, a protest against industrialized society, against . . .

I can't remember that very well anymore. It is peculiar, but now the distance from that period increases every day: entirely different things come into the foreground, the song of a blackbird in front of the window shortly after I have woken up and, somewhat further away, the crows in the trees, a water drop on a twig in the middle of the day after the thaw has begun. All that appears in a different light now, and everything which lies behind me I experience as insignificant.

She wove constantly; when we moved the biggest problem was always taking that loom apart and putting it back together. In the last apartment which we had together it reached almost up to the ceiling. She produced her own textile colors out of old plant dyes.

In Uppsala I had, after all, led a fairly wild life with girls and bars and debts. This new organic lifestyle in the country was one way of breaking with that permanently.

Certainly a romantic or perhaps anarchistic tendency

46

played a role in this. We both were disgusted with bureaucracy, with the centralization of this country, with the massive resettlement of human beings from their natural environment to impersonal, barracklike suburbs in large cities. We were disgusted by the school boards, which could not even manage to use the existing funds to make the schoolyards a bit more pleasant and friendly but instead spent the money on ostentatious sculptures. Through entire breakfasts we complained bitterly about the annexation of communities, about the closing of schools in sparsely settled areas, about the clear cutting of forests which made it quite evident that the entire area was being used like a warehouse for raw material, like a pantry one empties without restocking.

I mean: those were realities, those were things which meant something to us on a very practical, tangible level, perhaps there was also a bit of snobbishness in it, a feeling of being superior, of knowing better the significance of these events.

But there was something more: it gave us a kind of inner solidarity. When one knows everything better than the others, it is easy to stick together.

And we did stick together: in an unsentimental, not particularly sensual, but comfortable and good way. We experienced one another as two outsiders who had found one another and for whom individualism itself offered a common denominator; we were no longer outsiders because we had one another.

The fact that Margaret and I stuck together was a way of saying:

We begin again. We never give up.

She was the youngest daughter of an unbelievably tyrannical senior physician's family from Falun. All her brothers were officers in the reserve, Swedish masters of the military pentathlon, notaries, and God knows what else. I did not see them very often but had the impression that they viewed me with open contempt. One of them even asked me once whether one could really make a living as a grade school teacher—at that time the term "grade school teacher" was still used. We were totally incomprehensible to one another.

The father—he is, by the way, still alive I believe—was a horrible monster, feared by his family, by the nurses, by the subordinate doctors and assistants, known in the whole area for his medical pronouncements, which above all asserted that girls should wear woolen stockings in the winter, that abortion reduced the military strength of the country, and that the population was threatening to sink into an abyss of venereal disease and alcoholism among the young.

The youngest daughter had somehow gotten out of the clutches of this household. I have the impression that she spent the greater part of her youth making herself useful in the kitchen. In deathly fear of her father, suppressed by her brothers, pale, thin, and freckled, she had found her way to books, to a world outside of this twelve-room villa on the outskirts of Falun. I believe the path led through modern lyrics, which she began to read with curiosity, because once during lunch there had been some deprecating talk about them, and through the sarcastically quoted lines from Ekelöf and Lindegren she discovered that this somehow was about her:

"I seek a gold which eclipses all gold."

48

I believe she matured very late. She was about to be sent to a course in housekeeping when, for the first time in her life, she became really furious, stood up for herself, obtained a room in Uppsala, and registered at the university.

It was such an indescribably *Swedish* bourgeois family. Ten years later I could still hear traces of it in her speech.

This enormous, disdainful repugnance for everything which looked like personal intellectual work, this inimical attitude toward philosophy. "Education" consisted of being able to pronounce French words correctly. On the other hand it was considered "half-educated" to be interested in Marx, Kierkegaard, or Freud. That was acting like a grade school teacher.

Some of this was still present in her, in her cautious repugnance for everything that had the least appearance of "brooding."

I remember that I once actually argued with her about that to the point of being unable to talk to her at all for several days afterward. It was during a train trip to Copenhagen. (Sometimes we took such trips during our vacations.)

It began when I sketched out a thought which had been suggested to me by my reading.

—What if, now, I said, the word "I" were completely devoid of meaning? After all, the word "I" is used in everyday speech in precisely the same manner as the words "here" and "now." All people have the right to call themselves "I" and at the same time only one single person has that right, namely the one person speaking at that moment.

No one would assert that "here" or "there" means
49

something special, that it means something *exists* behind these concepts. Why should we then imagine we have an "I"?

It thinks in us. It feels. It talks. That is all. Or: It is thinking *here*, I said, and pressed my forefinger against my forehead.

—If you allow yourself to start brooding like that, you'll go crazy yet, she said.

(The Yellow Book II:8)

What a wonderful morning. Deep in my sleep, by the way, I was dreaming that a good-natured, nonetheless basically terribly dangerous elephant was chasing me across an endless field—but no pain tonight—deep in my sleep I felt that a tremendous blue high-pressure area had arrived. It lay over the whole region like a giant bubble when I got up at seven o'clock in the morning, and up to now not a single cloud has appeared, although it is afternoon already.

That is very unusual for March.

This morning I checked through all of the beehives already and filled up the sugar solution. As a matter of fact only one population froze. It is, however, one which had never demonstrated much spirit, I almost would have said. I have never really understood them. They built only about every second comb, and they did that in a hesitant, almost coquettish fashion, as if they wanted to say that they saw through these artificial wax combs, but they could nonetheless build a little bit if only to show that they at least had a command of geometry.

Coquettish beasts! I'm happy they froze. In the summer they would surely have been overcome with swarming fever, and then they would have destroyed themselves anyway. The idea of permanent revolution, so to speak.

Marengo, Austerlitz, Leipzig . . . I know few things which give rise to a Napoleonic complex to the same extent as does beekeeping. One can have all the experiences of a Napoleon without being cruel to horses and without seeing one single human being die.

Instead one sees a whole bunch of bees die.

Things could have continued like that for an indefinite

period of time: it was good, a harmony prevailed in the whole affair, a harmony at the cost of something, but nonetheless a harmony, yes, it could have continued like that.

If something had not begun to happen toward the end of the sixties. It came so unexpectedly that I virtually needed years in order to recognize what had happened. I was confronted with a radically new, completely unexpected event: love.

Naturally it took a catastrophic course, I had known that right from the beginning, but no catastrophe could actually frighten me. When I look back on how I acted, it truly looks as though I had *wanted* a catastrophe the whole time. It can hardly be interpreted any other way.

It is an unbelievably funny story, because it contains so very many improbable and peculiar chance occurrences.

I sometimes participated in these national meetings of the field biologists in Stockholm. And as I had been vice-chairman for several years, I had my way paid. So I used to stay on overnight in the Malmen Hotel and go to a concert or an opera in the evening. That was a small secret pleasure, and there really was nothing more to it.

Once, however, when we had such a meeting in October of 1969, I decided not to stay overnight, but to take the last train home. I really can't remember why.

I had checked my briefcase with the cloakroom attendant at the opera, left in the last intermission, and got to the train station just in time to get on the train which leaves at ten-forty for Oslo via Hallsberg and Västerås and which is usually full of American tourists traveling to Norway as well as a large number of more or less sober

52

people, who get off at Enköping and Västerås. Later on it really becomes more and more a night train.

I go into an almost completely full compartment and sit down. A fellow reeking of schnapps is sleeping to the left of me, one of those ugly camel's-hair coats pulled over his face, across from me several small, thin girls are sitting, possibly college students, and to the right of me in the window seat a fairly large blonde lady in her late thirties or early forties, apparently unmarried, who would have been ugly if it had not been for her wonderfully beautiful head.

Strangely enough, I began to talk with her, having barely come in, without actually looking up from the book which I had taken out of my briefcase, began to talk about how uncomfortable the cars in this train were, about train schedules, about the sleeping cars to Oslo and heaven knows what all—and the peculiar thing is that I didn't look up one single time. I spoke animatedly with her, continuing to read all the while in my book.

Only when we stopped in Kungsängen, and I wanted to step out of the compartment to check where we actually were, did I look at her.

She—how shall I say it—she radiated motherliness. Viewed externally there was nothing special about her, she was a bit chubby, but when I discovered her eyes, something peculiar . . . must have *happened*. These eyes *wanted* something from me, they made me more real, it had something to do with . . . (*two lines crossed out with ink*).

And then in Enköping, when I found out that at that hour there is no longer any connection to Tillberga and hesitated only a fraction of a second before I accepted her amazingly swift and friendly offer to take me there in her car in spite of the late hour—she was an assistant doctor in the Enköping hospital and thus used to odd hours—and the equally swift decision *not* to leave Enköping and then kisses, caresses, (a banal story, no, not a banal one at all), and the feeling of having been overwhelmed by something completely strange, to actually *change*, and this strange experience of sudden quiet.

As if one had come home.

Whether you believe me or not, an entire spring passed by before I saw her again, although we lived only sixty or seventy kilometers from one another. In this circumstance there was a kind of extravagance or a feeling of extravagant wealth.

Instead we would telephone one another late in the evening and talk about the events of the day. We wrote letters, very matter-of-fact, short letters containing little jokes.

Soon I knew the names of all the doctors and nurses and even the names of the most interesting patients on her ward in the Enköping hospital, and she knew pretty much everything about what was going on at my home. At my home nothing much was going on.

I was leading something like a double life, since I was so close to another life, which existed at a different place and in different surroundings, and perhaps I had needed precisely such a double life all along without knowing it.

(Always did have the suspicion that all solutions lie somewhere between my life and a different life.)

Perhaps the whole business could have settled itself and died down. We had slept once with one another, that was all right. Such things do happen, to some people they happen frequently, to others less frequently. We had slept once with one another, it had been very lovely, it had calmed me; I do not exclude the possibility that she at least originally did it with the intent of truly calming me. And things could have stayed that way.

But those eyes reminded me of something. They very simply awakened something in me.

They awakened the feeling in me that there was something tremendously important which I had always neglected up to then. (A banal story, no, not a banal one at all.) I discovered something in me which I had known nothing of. And I experienced that like a new beginning, it gave a new meaning to everything.

Naturally I made a really interesting mistake: I told Margaret about this affair.

(One could say, of course, that in time this was practically unavoidable, because there was no very plausible explanation for my sitting at the telephone every other evening for half an hour speaking between long pauses softly and at great length with someone who simply could not have been among our usual acquaintances.)

I had anticipated all kinds of reactions except the one that she would be glad. But that is exactly what happened. She was happy and relieved, as if someone had finally taken a much too great responsibility from her.

—Why don't you invite her over here, she said, meaning Ann. She would surely like to know how things look up here. She could come by sometime this summer, couldn't she? Does she have a car?

Naturally that was the beginning of the end, although at the time I didn't realize it.

55

I invited her for a Sunday in June. It was an unusually beautiful Sunday in June. I picked Ann up at the train station.

—The lake is very beautiful, she said. I had no idea that it was so large.

—I'm happy to see you again, I said.

—I don't know. I feel somewhat insecure.

—Why must people always act as if they were in novels, I said.

—Yes, presumably you're quite right, she said.

It was a very peculiar scene, seeing these two women together, Margaret small and thin, cool, Ann concerned and in a motherly way serious, as if she had come to see a patient whom she had to take care of. They knew nothing of one another, I was the only element which connected them.

In the first two minutes they appeared to be somewhat embarrassed in front of one another. This isn't going to work, I thought. It's going to be a terrible afternoon, I hope we can just get it behind us quickly. It is an insane undertaking that I have gotten into here.

As I said earlier: it was a radiantly beautiful Sunday morning in June 1970. All around us lay Västmanland. From a forest fire on one of the blue wooded mountain ridges in the north a faint, very aromatic scent of fire smoke wafted toward us. (Forest fires have the characteristic of having an extremely penetrating, unpleasant odor from close up, and at the distance of several kilometers an aromatic, pleasant one.)

Soft little gusts were moving across big Lake Åmänningen, wrinkling the water. In the northwest the pithead gears of shut-down mines were rusting away; the iron mines around Norberg haven't been profitable since the freight for African ore became cheaper. To the north a red cloud of smoke rose from a tapping at the Trummelsberg steelworks. From the canal and from the whole chain of lakes to the south came the sound of motorboats traveling back and forth on the many lakes.

It was the time of year during which the whole area suddenly becomes alive and populated. Whoever has experienced the winter quiet cannot believe that this is the same place. In winter the closest neighbor is the distant blinking light of a window six kilometers further away, on the other side of the lake.

To the south, the belt of damper and damper, swampier and swampier woods which divided us from the valley of Lake Mälar, the church of Ramnäs with its characteristic bulbous steeple, Ramnäs, where my poor alcoholic Uncle Knutte would always return after once again having tried to pedal through the woods in a thundershower to reach the liquor store in Västerås, the plain which at the black, quiet little river Kolbäcksan ultimately opens in the direction of Sörstafors and Kolbäck, the region in which my unhappy romantic Aunt Clara traveled around during one notable fall shortly after the Second World War with an old, blind, bearded vagabond, with whom she had fallen head over heels in love—she died of pneumonia shortly afterwards, the poor thing. We are a strange family. We do strange things.

And there I was standing, introducing my wife to a lady who apparently was the great love of my life.

They went intently along the garden paths looking at

the flower beds. (At that time, in the year 1970, this house was a vacation cottage.)

—Watch out for the bees, I said. They are having a restless period right now. They are pretty aggressive.

They only laughed.

The garden is very small really. One doesn't need long to look at it. They were taking their time.

They came back, giggling and a little exhilarated. They had found one another.

Bees and bumblebees were humming around, the church bells were ringing over in Väster Våla, it was, as has been said before, a truly wonderful summer day.

—Utopia, I thought. Utopia has become reality. I always suspected it. Nothing really keeps us from living outside the normal rules of life. Why didn't I realize this long ago!

Then there followed a fairly strange period. I think it changed us very much, me, Ann, but most of all Margaret.

I had never really realized that she needed a mother.

(The Yellow Book II:10)

Everybody probably knows from their own experience the uncomfortable feeling one has at a train station. One wants to say goodbye to somebody. The person from whom one wants to take leave has already gotten on the train, but the train simply does not start up. There one stands now, one on the platform, the other behind the window, both trying to talk with one another, but suddenly there is not another word to say.

Naturally that has to do with the fact that we are no longer permitted to experience what we want. The situation dictates a feeling. And who has not experienced this tremendous relief when the train finally leaves the station?

Or at burials? When someone dies, gets sick, when there are disappointments, very definite feelings are expected of us. In every situation except for the most everyday, most neutral ones, a pressure is exerted as to how we are to behave, how we are to feel. And when one looks at the matter a little more closely, one discovers not infrequently that novels, films, and theater pieces which one has seen or read somewhere have dictated these roles for us.

When reality confronts us with unusual situations (for example, when an anticipated rivalry doesn't materialize and instead there is a love which excludes us), we first reach for these emotional stereotypes common to novels.

They don't give us much footing. They make us lonelier than before, and head over heels we fall out into reality.

(The Blue Book II:5)
59

It took me a rather long time during that strange summer of 1970 to realize how Ann was being taken away from me.

(And I think that in doing so they took from me my last chance for achieving independence, for achieving a clarity about myself and my own dimensions, for which I had been destined all my life, toward which everything had pointed.

What the two women succeeded in blocking was an eruption of reality, of personality.)

I imagine the matter this way:

The fact that I was married released in Ann a whole complex of guilt feelings. They did not square with the fact that she loved me just as much as I her. At the same time she was oriented by her whole upbringing and all her ideals to see guilt feelings as harmful, as evil.

She turned them into "sympathetic feelings" for Margaret. Margaret for her part immediately saw her opportunity, and together they turned me into something irresponsible, into a child upon which one couldn't really rely.

They led me around by the nose, because this triad of various motherly and sisterly relationships created such a warmth, such a peace as I had never experienced, neither before that time nor afterward.

Like the warmth of a bird's nest.

(The Blue Book II:6)

3. A Childhood

Since the pains got serious, something peculiar has been happening:

Completely different stages in life, completely different memories have taken on the greatest importance for me.

Marriage, professional life, oh God! All that is vanishing as if it were a trifle, a short episode, everything which just a short time ago would fill the whole world and would keep me awake during the night sometimes with melancholy speculations. All that is becoming an episode in a much more important story in which, up to this point, my childhood is the only really significant chapter.

I don't quite understand why that is so. Childhood is, though, a lonely, an egocentric age, and perhaps pain is making me lonely again and egocentric like a child.

This constant concern with an indefinite, dangerous secret in one's own body, this feeling that some dramatic change is taking place, without one's being able to have any clarity about what it really is, in a perverse fashion all that reminds me of prepuberty. I even recognize this gentle feeling of shame again.

When I burnt this damned letter I somehow took the whole matter upon myself. I will have to fight alone, and I will have my own death.

But still I don't believe in it. It is very possible that by April everything will have changed. If it's kidney stones, they are going to be passed sooner or later. If it's an infection, then it may certainly fade away as soon as the weather gets somewhat warmer and friendlier.

I simply feel much too vital to be dying. I imagine death to be something much more foggy, much feebler.

A dying person can't take long walks with the dog in between attacks of pain.

Or is this perhaps a new kind of dying which I'm inventing?

To fill the measure of misfortune, the outer world has begun to announce itself for the first time in months.

The chief of the regional tax administration, Söderkvist, the carpenter, called, very friendly and amenable, by the way, in order to point out to me that a penalty will be due if I do not submit my tax statement. My cousin and his family, the Manngårdhs, want to stop by at Easter on their way to Sälen, stay overnight here, and "have a look around," as they say.

That could get out of hand.

I told Söderkvist that I wasn't feeling too well at the moment. He promised to stop by one of the next evenings in order to help me.

It really is, as he said on the telephone, not a particularly difficult tax statement. We will certainly get it done in less than an hour.

"To fill the measure of misfortune"—such phrases take me back instantaneously to my childhood. That period reverberated with such phrases.

"To fill the measure of misfortune" means naturally that something extra has been added to the misfortune. There is so much misfortune that it threatens to overflow.

TO FILL THE MEASURE OF MISFORTUNE— that was one of the things my mother would say.

Aunt Svea would have expressed it in a completely different way. She would have said: IT CAN HAPPEN THAT ONE GETS PREGNANT WITH A NIGGER BABY.

THE DEVIL HAS A HAND IN THAT GAME— Papa.

64

WHY DON'T YOU KISS MY ASS—Uncle Stig.
DEVIL'S BLOOD AND THE TEARS OF THE UN-
BORN
CURSES AND DAMNATION
OH NO, HE BIT GRANDPA IN THE LEG

I see her in the summer in the country at the breakfast table, usually there are several relatives there WHO HAVE INTRUDED. Uncle Knutte, a bit bald-headed, with wobbling, quivering jowls, always somewhat sweaty at breakfast as if he really couldn't stand it, always very quiet, apart. Uncle Stig with a short, square-cut beard and gold-rimmed glasses speaks only of metal alloys and the most recent successes of Russian technology in the Korean War. Of tanks, which in spite of their thin armor stand up to American rocket bombs. Of the possibility of utilizing the warmth from the earth's core when fossil fuels begin to play out. Aunt Svea, tall, with crimson cheeks and rough hands, which feel like sandpaper when she pats one's face, tells fantastic stories of the restaurant kitchens of the crisis period: of thin, bluish fox carcasses with their paws hacked off, which are delivered very discreetly at seven o'clock in the morning at the back entrance by the kitchen door, of the heavy pan with the farmers' breakfast, which is handed around until very slowly a thick, gray layer of solid fat builds up on its surface, and of the drunken lumber merchant who drops one of his suspenders into the toilet and then, in an orderly fashion, puts it back on over his elegant black-market nylon shirt without noticing a thing and then has to be taken home discreetly in a taxi.

Aunt Clara—no, she is not there anymore. Grandma

Emma was never along, never belonged to that group, was not even a real grandmother, but only an adoptive grandmother and died when I was three years old. I only know of her from the things people say. (How in the world did I happen to think of her—something is happening to my memory, something strange that I would not have thought possible, things begin to crop up in it, things I would never have thought could even be there. For several days a memory has been haunting me which must go back to the time before my third birthday; with Grandma Emma, who is holding me by the hand, I am walking under colossally tall green trees on the Djäkneberg in Västeras, the shadows of foliage flutter on the ground in maelstroms, yes, really in maelstroms. And the fact that all this is happening at an incredibly early time is substantiated only by the tremendous height of the park benches.)

ANOTHER

This expression is one of the most peculiar, bizarre ways of saying "I" in the Swedish language. It is colloquial speech, but much more interesting than the colloquialism is, naturally, the philosophy behind it. ANOTHER— that is, a fencer who springs aside at the last moment and lets the sword of the opponent pierce empty air where someone just stood.

I cannot imagine a stranger, more ghostly language than one in which it is possible to speak of oneself as if one were someone else.

—"ANOTHER" HAD TO GET HIMSELF THROUGH ON HIS OWN MOST OF THE TIME, YOU KNOW.

That means: you didn't do very much to help me, you actually have a lot to do with my problems, it's not certain at all that without you I would even have had these problems. Therefore, you owe me a LARGE DEBT OF GRATITUDE.

—EVERYONE IS THE MASTER OF HIS OWN DESTINY (Uncle Stig thunders from the other end of the table).

That means: it is your own fault that you are half an alcoholic.

TO FILL THE MEASURE OF MISFORTUNE.

It is strange, but however often I rummage around in my memories of all the conversations which I heard in my childhood, not a one occurs to me in which a single participant was excluded from playing out more or less subtle guilt feelings. These feelings of guilt were comparable to the ball in a tennis game.

Without these guilt feelings their relationships would have ossified, rigid like petrified statues. There would have been no driving force, no motivation anymore.

The feeling of guilt was the tensed spring in the rachet, the reply the little pawl which released it.

These guilt feelings encompassed a huge, a truly church-organlike register, beginning with

WILL YOU PLEASE PASS ME THE SALT

in the highest register, over

IT WOULD BE VERY NICE IF YOU WOULD LEAVE A LITTLE BIT OF THE SUGAR

somewhere between the sesquialtera and the two-footed pipe flute, down to the growling, deep, thirty-two foot basses like

SINCE I SACRIFICED EVERYTHING FOR YOU

or

IF IT HADN'T BEEN FOR YOU, WE WOULD HAVE GOTTEN A DIVORCE AFTER THE FIRST YEAR

These last, extremely deep voices naturally were used only to achieve very special effects. For church holidays, so to speak.

What kind of strange fugues, toccatas, ricercari, passacaglias they could play on this peculiar organ of guilt, what depths of small peasant fear did they conjure up, of infamous exchanges of dirty linen. It took them only one single run over the keyboard to have somebody hanging wriggling in the net.

DO YOU KNOW, PAPA ALWAYS LOVED ME THE BEST OF ALL THE BROTHERS AND SISTERS

DO YOU KNOW, STIG ALWAYS WAS MAMA'S FAVORITE, HE WAS SUCH A HARDWORKING LITTLE BOY

They hadn't had easy lives, not particularly dramatic, and certainly not tragic (it was, after all, in the forties, during which a great many real tragedies were unleashed in the world; one must maintain some sense of proportion), but God knows nothing had ever happened to them for which they could not somehow blame one another. And that gave them a marvelous opportunity of making things unpleasant for one another, to maneuver one another into the desired positions.

68

The lower middle class in Sweden lives from guilt and self-denigration, they only know one form of rhetoric, namely the complaint.

RELEASE FINALLY YOUR SUFFERING HU-MANITY

BUT FIRST OF ALL ME, BECAUSE I HAVE SUF-FERED THE MOST

One only needs to go a few kilometers on the commuter train to see how it is. If they don't have any other reason for complaining, they complain about their cursed ill-nesses, their aching knees, their gallstones and stomach ulcers, their swollen varicose veins, their hiccups and their heartburn, their diarrhea and their stone-hard turds clattering into the chamber pots and at the same time they always imagine *somebody will be concerned about them,* if only they complain. THESE DAMNED IDIOTS

Right now, for example, I feel a pulsing pain, which in a few minutes is going to keep me from finishing these sentences. It begins pretty far down somewhere in the right calf, where it feels something like liquid metal, or like something which has hooked into the musculature, a golden wire one could perhaps say. Then it radiates to the right loin, sends, along the back of the leg, a whole bundle of white radiating gold wires to the navel and the hip, and a fan of this radiating gold extends up to the diaphragm. When I lie down, it hurts twice as much; when I remain seated, it wanders up to the back, it doesn't always maintain the same pitch, the frequencies, the decibel count of this white radiating gold changes

69

constantly, they create chords, very clean, clear chords, until they suddenly get tangled somehow and become *cutting*.

But, dammit, I do not *blame* anybody for that! *Nobody*!

Much better for the past three days. There is still a little pain, that's all.

Funny, yesterday I made two friends. That hasn't happened to me in a long time.

One's called Uffe, the other Jonny. Uffe is twelve years old, Jonny is going to be twelve soon.

Uffe is from Skinnskatteberg and Jonny from Borgå in Finland. Just as I went outside to look for the mail, there they were in front of the door, almost exactly alike in their hooded blue windbreakers, a little freckled, long-haired like horses.

I think they live in this lumberjack community up there near Sörby; their parents moved there last fall. They attend the Trummelsberg Central School, but naturally they had no idea that I once was a teacher there.

They were looking for some kind of adventure, after school I hope, but it is not to be ruled out that with the lovely weather they had simply skipped a day and then got thirsty and wanted to have a drink of water.

But I assume that more than anything else they knocked out of pure curiosity. They simply wanted to know what kind of a strange person it is who lives in the little house behind a lot of bushes and the long row of green beehives.

—Come in, I said.

They were a bit shy. I told them something about the

bees, but that didn't seem to interest them particularly.

Then we talked for a time about their parents: apparently their fathers have been hired on for some of the big clearings which, I understand, are now getting under way.

They didn't have a lot to say about school; no, eating in the cafeteria is more pleasant than in their previous schools, they said, because here the trays aren't made of metal, and for that reason there's not such a fantastic amount of noise. One of them wanted to learn how to play ice hockey, the other was interested in basketball.

Little by little they thawed out in the warmth of my electric heater and cautiously began to play around with the dog. Jonny's socks were completely wet, he probably had holes in his boots (it is an absolute mystery to me anyway how he can run around at this time of year in rubber boots), and I suggested that I could let him use a pair of my old wool socks or that I could give them to him. A bit hesitantly he accepted the offer and opened his school bag in order to put in his own wet ones (I had wrapped them for him in a piece of newspaper).

Thus I discovered that he was dragging around a tremendous number of pulp digests, all of them pretty much read to pieces. I asked him if I could take a look at them; it was a surprisingly large bundle for such a small school bag, all of them horror magazines of the worst sort: THE GRAVE PERSON, KUNG FU, ICE COLD THRILLERS, THE FANTASTIC FOUR and the like.

We leafed around in them together. It was really interesting.

—Why do you read this kind of thing?

71

They couldn't explain that.

I almost think I could explain it. It is the obscure, droning fear of prepuberty, which has to focus itself somewhere. It seeks points for crystallization. One could almost call it the horror phase. Thus we sat there with the clock ticking away and talked about ghosts and Danish bog corpses and about the possible existence of terrible monsters on strange planets, until the dog began to yowl because he had to go pee badly and I noticed that I had missed my usual mealtime.

They were very happy, I think. Before they went, they promised to come back soon. And I promised them that by that time I would make up a much better horror story for them than these pathetic commercial pulps could offer.

These little fellows have made me perk up somehow. They have reminded me of myself. Also, I am beginning to ask myself whether it was a premature decision to give up teaching. But first of all it's not particularly amusing to get up every winter morning at six o'clock and try to start the car, and second it is rather late to be thinking about that now.

(The Yellow Book III:1–4)

The Great Organ on the Island Og

Up to now the following has taken place: the fraternal order on the mainland of Tinth has sent Dick Roger in a boat to the Islands of Fog. These islands have been under the control of the evil magician Emperor Ming for over a year, although everyone had thought that he perished in flames and smoke when, at the end of the last story, his black tower hurtled into a hole in the universe which he himself had created. Recently ships have disappeared in the straits of Tinth, a thick, unnatural fog envelops the islands, and the fraternal order fears that the Grand Master's niece, the beautiful Diana Din, who but a short time before had been kidnapped by several fearsome, black-clad men in leather masks, is possibly being held prisoner there.

On one of the most distant islands Dick Roger comes upon two Finnish sailors, both frightened to death, whose becalmed ship was suddenly whirled in the air by a peculiar cyclone. He gives them food and dry socks. The sailors have terrible things to relate.

Ming maintains his occupation of the islands through the help of his inhuman henchmen, who, according to the reports of all refugees, are invincible and possess supernatural powers; probably they are demons. The islands themselves are enveloped in a magical fog.

Presumably Ming keeps Diana Din imprisoned in his subterranean caverns, where he is working on his newest horrifying invention: a giant organ, which with its peculiar high-frequency sounds can influence the psyche of human beings and which by means of electromagnetic oscillations can cause them to experience pain even at great distances.

In a little house on a small rock island just off the coast Dick Roger and his companions find a strange white-bearded old man named Sigismund, who maintains that he possesses an infallible cure for the terrible effects of the giant organ.

The cure involves a magical snake, and the old man stubbornly insists that they must take it along in a clay jug.

After a terrible storm the seafarers reach the foggy coast of OG.

Although it had to be well into the forenoon, a deep darkness enveloped everything. Between the veils of fog which were moving back and forth restlessly as if they were living beings, the high black cliffs of the coast appeared. Above their crest, an endless stream of clouds was passing low and quickly—like an army, thought Dick, an army of restless spirits.

The breakers were getting smaller now. The storm, which had raged so violently during the night, was being replaced by a gentle breeze.

He looked back for a brief moment. The exhausted sailors in their ragged and torn leather jackets were unloading the rest of the provisions and lowering the sails from the ship, which quite obviously would not endure the stress of the storm much longer.

The only one who gave the impression of being completely calm was Sigismund; with his clay jug and his rug he had sat down on a spot of dry sand very near the black, steep shore cliffs. The place, the time, and the situation didn't seem to disturb him any more than if he had been taking a lovely Sunday afternoon walk.

At this moment he pulled out a beautiful silver flute from a hidden fold of the torn coatlike garment which he wore. He polished the flute carefully on the arm of the garment, until even in this strange November twilight it glowed with a peculiar illumination.

Apparently he had opened the top of the clay jug, which, strangely enough, had not been broken in the rough landing. He put the flute to his lips. A strange wailing melody sounded through the howling of the wind.

—He is playing for the snake, thought Dick.

The two Finnish sailors, yes, they had said only the moment before the precipitous landing that they were really Finnish sailors who had been left stranded several years ago in this part of the country after a shipwreck, were gathering wood for a fire.

—I'm wondering whether that's smart, said Dick and pointed to the wood. Someone could see it very clearly through the fog.

The Finnish sailors nodded thoughtfully. The head of the snake now appeared over the top of the clay jug. It was weaving back and forth.

—The snake is dancing, Dick said, more to himself than to the others, Yes, it's really dancing!

At the same moment he felt a cutting, knifing pain. It originated from a point in his right thigh. Dick looked around quickly. He saw how all around him the others,

75

too, were bent up in pain. One of the Finnish sailors, apparently in convulsions, was writhing on the ground. The only creature who seemed completely unaffected was the strange snake in its jug.

The pains were worse than he had ever thought possible.

—There's only one hope, said Dick, who summoned up all his strength just to say anything at all. The terrible organ must have been finished two weeks earlier than we anticipated.

We must find the place where these vibrations originate!

(The Blue Book III:1)

"Malignant growths occur when a cell, a group of cells, or a tissue disassociates itself from its environment and forms an independent entity which lives from the rest of the organism. Morphologically these growths exhibit a disorderly and purposeless structure similar to that of embryonic tissue; their cells exhibit an abnormal structure of irregular, very differentiated appearance. A malignant growth grows rapidly and independently from the rest of the organism. With its growth it destroys the surrounding normal tissue, to some extent by means of the pressure which occurs due to its expansion, but primarily by immediate destruction. The growth penetrates the neighboring intercellular spaces, the blood cells, and the lymph cells in part by means of hairlike plasma extensions, in part, however, by scattering single cells or small particles into the blood and lymph system. These embed themselves in a more distant organ and form new tumor centers, which have the same destructive characteristics as the mother tumor."

> (The Blue Book: Copied out of
> a book which is not identified,
> III:16)

After yesterday's events it is clear to me that I have not taken the pain seriously up to now. I have only played with it. One could almost say that I have let it give me a new meaning in life—the change between the days on which there was no pain and the days on which there was pain was very dramatic.

There was something, after all, which one could hope for every morning on awakening, and every evening on going to bed one was again and again just as expectant about whether the night would be free of pain. Occasionally, periods of two, three, up to four days passed during which I didn't feel anything at all in this peculiar place in the right loin.

The pain dramatized the fact that I have a body, no, that I *am* a body, and from this fact that I am a body, a peculiar consolation, almost a security, could be drawn, almost like a very lonely person draws security from the presence of a pet.

This pet was very problematic and especially toward morning rather resembled a wild animal, but, in any case, it somehow belonged to *me*, just as the pain belonged to *me* and to no one else.

But now I'm beginning to wonder what I have let myself in for, when, for instance, I burned that letter without opening it.

What I have experienced today during the late night and in the early hours of the morning, *I simply could not have considered possible.* It was absolutely foreign, white hot and totally overpowering. I am trying to breathe very slowly, but as long as it continues, even this breathing, which at least in some very abstract fashion is supposed to help me distinguish between the physical pain and the panic, is an almost overpowering exertion.

A far cry from a pet now. A terrible, unheard of, white hot, impersonal power is taking its residence in my nervous system, occupies it to the last molecule and tries to explode every nerve into a cloud of blinding white gases, as in—in the corona of the sun (the whole night I thought about sun protuberances, the way they pulse, the way they break forth in cascades on the surface of the sun).

I recognize that I took the whole thing too lightly. I did not take it seriously enough, just like everything else in this life.

But this comes from outside! My God, where does it come from? And what incredible secret powers a poor, suffering nervous system can produce, powers which are exclusively directed against me. Against me, of all people.

Now it has become somewhat better again. For the past few hours it has really been better. But I still have a cold sweat, and the pencil shakes in my hand when I try to write.

I hope, no, I am absolutely certain that it will never come back, certainly something has been destroyed, so absolutely destroyed that it will never hurt again.

But perhaps it will return in just a few hours?

What I experience is total dissolution, total confusion.

Up to now I never really grasped that the possibility of experiencing ourselves as something clearly defined, or-dered, as a human self depends on the possibility of a future. The foundation of the entire concept of the self is that it will continue to exist tomorrow.

79

This white hot pain, naturally, is basically nothing but a precise measure of the forces which hold this body together. It is a precise measure of the force which has made my existence possible. Death and life are actually MONSTROUS things.

(The Yellow Book III:23)

"Asta Bolin didn't claim to know an answer to the question whether suffering has a meaning. The topic of the lecture had been formulated more to beg the question.

Nonetheless, she had many valuable words to offer, words of consolation, words of meaning.

She told how once, when a friend in a deep state of grief experienced absolute meaninglessness, she, in her inability to deal with the situation, said some words which were a genuine help to him. These words were: 'Everything takes on that meaning which we ourselves give it.'

Asta Bolin didn't want these words taken as some kind of philosophical or other kind of truth, but she said they indeed expressed something very essential: that one can approach one's grief actively, that one can work on it."

(The Yellow Book: A newspaper clipping from the *Vestmanlands Läns Tidning*, March 10, III:26)

Bogs. Swampland. Slow, lazy waters fanning out into many small channels. Birds taking to the air hastily in a single cloud when one approaches them. Gentle winds wrinkling the deep, brown water. Clouds.

I spent a large portion of my childhood summers south of the woods, near the ironworks of Ramnäs.

It is strange, but always when I need consolation, not a fleeting, casual, but a deep consolation, a consolation which tells you that nothing will be better and that you must nonetheless feel consoled—then this region comes back to my mind.

And everything is a single sound of flowing water, almost everywhere. From the black whirlpools of the locks at Färmansbo down to the strangely sad, bird-rich swamp areas on Lake Norra Nadden.

The fish swarm which stands totally still in the shallow water and disappears with lightning swiftness when a shadow falls on it.

In the little river Kolbäcksån somewhere between the lakes, my father and I almost drowned once when we tried, on a day very late in November 1943, to row across it in order to buy some butter at a farmer's. It was an old brown rowboat of the kind used by farmers—but only south of Lake Åmänningen, where the bottoms are smooth as glass from the algae which grow on them, in other areas the boats aren't as flat-bottomed—in such a boat one can break his neck if one doesn't pay attention moving around, and besides that it leaks like the devil.

The boat we had borrowed leaked terribly, much more than we had anticipated, and we had to keep taking turns bailing like crazy, with aching arms, before we landed at the last moment on a mud bar on the other bank. The water was ice cold and my hands were completely blue.

Little though I was this bailing process appeared to me, I now think, to be a symbol of life.

The black market played an enormous role in my life as a small boy. I had the impression that we were constantly about on evening expeditions to buy butter without ration cards or to purchase pieces of a moose.

For the past three days the pain has been flowing more weakly. It is as if it had gotten through some terrible waterfall, and as if we had now reached a kind of backwater again, in the black, lazy eddies on the other side. Yesterday I went walking again a little bit. I didn't dare to drive the car, I feel a little too weak for that, but since Sundblad is here over the February vacation and knows that I am not particularly well, my shopping has been done for me every day at the grocery store. I only wonder how things are going to be when the Sundblads are gone again. Probably I'll get back on my feet. Deep down I have the feeling of having withstood a kind of crisis: I just feel pretty wrung out. I am telling myself, whether rightly so or not, that it's something like a tumor that had to rupture and has ruptured, and now that it has, I must automatically be on the way to improvement. I hope that that is true.

In any case it must have cost me a lot of strength. Whatever happened last week. Whatever it was. All morning long I wondered whether I should put the ladder up to the attic to take down a couple of frames for the beehives which have to be sanded and newly varnished. Then I would have had something meaningful to do; this writing just makes me more depressed. But having considered the matter all morning long, I came to the conclusion that I simply couldn't do it.

Perhaps tomorrow.

The clouds have always been low over this swampland and mirrored in the water, in the channels.

In those summers—particularly in the summers of the forties—I sometimes had the feeling of walking under a roof. As if I had gotten into some complicated trap.

Then, in the forties, there were still those farmers' kitchens with huge, white-chalked ovens. On every holiday they would be whitewashed with a new layer of chalk, with the years they must have grown with all those additional layers of chalk.

It must have been next to such a huge, white-tiled, warm oven that my father and I ended our adventure that time. I still recall the taste of the thin coffee, tasting almost burnt, which we used to drink then.

On the crest of one of those high hills on the west side of Lake Åmänningen, where at that time an old, steep gravel road led from Fagersta to Virsbo, my Uncle Sune had a store.

A green house with a gasoline pump in front of it, a large, red gasoline pump of this truly fascinating kind with a glass bowl on top in which one could see the yellow gasoline turn a screw. In the forties, naturally, there was no gasoline in the pump, but it looked snappy anyway. On the upper floor my uncle lived together with his unbelievably fat wife, Ruth, whom one never saw outside; I believe she even had difficulties getting down the stairs to the store, where she presided with a tremendous, somewhat blood-spotted butcher apron in front of her round belly.

The store was completely brown inside, brown walls, brown counter, from the brown counter a brown cord extended out of a hole, which someone must have made with a crowbar. That was long before the time of plastic bags. A meat counter made out of glass, where several greenish slices of liver were floating around in an indefinable organic liquid. In the back a small room, in which Uncle Sune counted ration cards half the night long, the glasses with the steel rims pushed up on his forehead, in the yard a shed with petroleum, hardware, several of the strictly rationed bicycle tires, and other small items.

He always smoked, small, brown cigarillos, and since he had a little mustache of a model similar to Nietzsche's or Stalin's, one was always somewhat concerned that this mustache would catch fire as the cigarillo stub glowed down slowly like an old-fashioned fuse.

Perhaps he had yet other similarities to Nietzsche as well. He was an individualist. He wouldn't let himself be impressed. In discussions about wartime events, which would take place in front of his counter while he was running back and forth with the cigarillo stub in the corner of his mouth, a pencil stuck behind each ear, and a scissors for the rationing cards tied to his belt with a string, always in a hurry, he would take the stub out of his mouth for just a second to whisper:

85

—It's always the same old shit!

"It's always the same old shit" was almost for him a kind of motto, a response which he utilized in all somewhat dramatic moments.

He had a truck, a Volvo, with a wood-burner in one of the sheds in the yard behind that house on the gravel road. Sometimes the car ran, sometimes it didn't. It took hours to cut the wood for the burner, little pieces of a special shape, which one hacked out of round pieces which had been prepared with a broad-toothed saw. It was hellishly tiresome to prepare the fire in the burner, it was a real test of patience until the gas began to flow as it was supposed to into the various channels and cavities of the peculiar high pot behind the driver's compartment. Sometimes it really started to burn in there, and then one had to get to the nearest lakeshore immediately—there were many, thank God—and pour water over the whole apparatus. And the cylinders were always sticky and smeared with dark-brown tar.

But he absolutely needed the car to get flour and sugar and milk cans and strange things from Västerås and Kolbäck, which could only be transported by night.

Uncle Sune dealt in a lot of things. He did that, by the way, until late into the sixties, but by then, of course, he had been in the construction business for a long time and belonged to those who got state loans for rental property. This property would then be thrown up, covering whole fields in Hallstahammar and Virsbo, and rented to Finnish industrial workers for exorbitant prices; their houses sprouted up in that region the way mushrooms do from the moist Västmanland loam. But that is, actually, a completely different story. At that time he was already in Västerås in an eighteen-room villa with a swimming pool and a copper roof and called himself a contractor.

But this was in the forties.

In the summer of 1940, Sune located three large barrels of first-class gasoline. He got them out of Norway of all places, I don't know how that was possible, but probably he traded something else for them.

The motor of the truck was too run-down to have it pay to convert it again to a gasoline engine, but he still had his old Plymouth, a prewar model, which had been on blocks for two whole years in the shed of a neighboring farm.

He dragged it home with two horses and spent a Saturday and a Sunday putting it back in shape. The motor hummed like a cat on the excellent German airplane fuel which, in some inexplicable fashion, had managed to get over the Norwegian border, which at that time not even refugees could cross.

Naturally, it was quite clear that he could not, without further ado, travel around with normal gasoline. That would have brought him behind bars in the shortest possible time. His neighbors were envious and grudging enough already.

Almost every one of them, even though he had given them credit for months. To say nothing of all sorts of shady deals with the valuable ration cards, deals which he would always let go by unnoticed. This ingrate pack that was always slandering him. Always the same old shit!

He found an auto repair shop near Sörstafors which

87

had a wood-burner for sedans. They installed it on a small trailer and connected it to the car by means of a complicated system of hoses, pipes, rods, and ball joints. The wood-burner was completely covered with rust and damaged by fire, but it still had one quality: it could roll on wheels.

Uncle Sune bought it as scrap for five crowns, brought it home on the truck, and spent an entire weekend painting this monstrosity silver bronze. As long as one didn't scratch the paint, it looked fantastic.

The car ran like clockwork on this gasoline, and the burner hobbled behind on the trailer as well as it could. Naturally it slowed the speed a little, but otherwise the car drove just like a prewar vehicle.

Uncle Sune traveled around half of Västmanland, enjoyed his new freedom of movement in great measure, drove his plump wife to a cinema in Västerås, and found life comfortable all along the line. This was a period, by the way, in which business was fantastic.

The old country road between Virsbo and Fagersta was not in particularly good repair. Today an asphalt road goes right across Uncle Sune's farmyard, nothing remains of the green grocery store, the only reminder of the old place is an unusually beautiful, old ash tree, which in some wondrous way has withstood the caterpillar tractors and explosions and now bends over the right lane.

Every time I drive by I think of those times. And every new spring the ash puts out leaves.

They are strong trees, the ashes.

The old road would have bad potholes in the middle after the wood hauls of the winter. In early spring it could happen that an entire piece of the left shoulder (I always see the landscape from north to south, but I am used to the fact that most of the time we would travel in the other direction) falls into Lake Åmanningen, and then warning stakes of the highway department announced in glowing red colors, here one must be careful. There were unbelievable slopes, the longest of which was certainly five kilometers long, a veritable paradise for every bicycle rider coming from the north, and a nightmare for those coming from the south.

The new street is almost completely flat. In these mighty chains of hills, the foothills of the Landsberg, it runs through tremendous incisions created by blasts, and the old, reed-covered swamps in the Lake Södra Nadden region with their wind-wrinkled channels, their wild ducks and mysterious labyrinths of lazy, black waters, have been filled up partially with thousands of wagon-loads of the fill material from these explosions. The landscape has been turned inside out.

Perhaps this landscape has lost its soul. Perhaps it is only hiding it. I believe that one day it will return.

Be that as it may: at that time, in the spring of 1942, or 1943, the road was in terrible condition, and after an exchange of letters lasting about half a year, the two communities of Virsbo and Västanfors got the provincial government in Västerås to make a road inspection.

The gentlemen from the provincial government started early in the morning in two completely full cars, running, as might be expected, on wood-burners. At the intersection north of Virsbo the deputation met with the representatives of the Virsbo community (I am going by the account in the *Vestmanlands Läns Tidning*), who joined them in a third car.

So it was an exceptionally felicitous demonstration that the last car, occupied by the Road Administration Director and the Secretary of the Provincial Government, who also held an equally high position in the Rationing Bureau, broke its axle three kilometers south of Uncle Sune's hill. Together with two assessors of the provincial government, they had to wade through the early spring slush until they came to Uncle Sune's house. It was an additional misfortune that they had been at the end of the column when the calamity occurred, and the people in the two other cars had apparently not noticed it.

They stomped through the slush, carrying on a lively discussion about whether they ought to go in the direction of Fagersta or return to Virsbo, and in the middle of their debate the Secretary of the Provincial Government caught sight of Uncle Sune's red gasoline pump on top of the hill.

In the meantime sweat was running down his red face, and his woolen scarf, which he had put into his pocket, dragged like a train behind him. Thank heavens one of the assessors had relieved him of his briefcase.

Uncle Sune knew the Road Administration Director as well as the Secretary of the Provincial Government through the *Vestmanlands Läns Tidning*, and for a moment he paled. Had one of his more profitable business doings in recent times been perhaps a trifle too daring?

When he saw the condition they were in, he calmed

down again quickly and under the Stalin mustache smiled his most winning smile.

Soon the gentlemen were sitting in their underwear at a coffee table on the second floor, while next door in the kitchen Ruth was working on their pants with a steaming-hot iron. The conversation revolved around the terrible condition of the road, truly a car broke its rear axle every other day, and around the difficulties a poor merchant had in this time of crisis with the calculation of the ration coupons, and of course the gentlemen understood, between us, Mr. Jansson, it simply isn't that easy to sit in the Gas Rationing Bureau and perhaps a small, a very small cognac would be in order?

It was tremendously pleasant, and it could have gone on like that until far into the night. It was completely clear to the Road Administration Director that the street had to be asphalted with all possible speed, at least to this truly nice little store, and everything was peace and joy, until one of the gentlemen chanced to cast his gaze upon his watch.

Panic! Pants on quick, the heartiest thanks, and now the only question is, dear Mr. Jansson, whether you could possibly be so kind as to drive us—to Virsbo or to Västanfors—but, by the way, which of the two is closer?

—Ah so, to Västanfors? But dear Mr. Jansson, you have already been so kind, really, and now you even go so far as to drive us all the way to Västanfors. You have just got your new wood-burner operating as I heard?

Uncle Sune crept out to the petroleum shed and gassed up the Plymouth.

The trip was just as pleasant as the whole afternoon.

Uncle Sune was in his very best mood, the cigarillo was nimbly swinging up and down his Nietzsche mustache, and by the time they got to the Alcoholics' Institute at Sundby, he had virtually finalized a special allocation of textiles for his store from the Gas Rationing Bureau. Triumphantly the car drove up in front of the old town hall of Fagersta, where a melancholy reception committee cheered up somewhat when they caught sight of the gentlemen in the back seat. They were the councilmen from three communities, gentlemen from the provincial legislature, and from the Road Administration, and the Västanfors Police Chief.

The gentlemen climbed out and expressed thanks for the ride. Simultaneously someone discovered that the wood-burner was missing. It simply was not there! Either Uncle Sune had forgotten to connect it in his haste or more probably the silly thing had torn loose on the trip.

He was just as genuinely astonished as all the others.

—Well, my goodness, said Sune, where is my wood-burner?

The car puttered along merrily on empty, but no one—thank God—had enough presence of mind to notice that.

—We must have lost that piece of shit on the way, said Sune.

But how in heaven's name did we manage to get here? asked the Road Administration Director.

—Really, that's very simple, said the Secretary of the Provincial Government, with the full weight and the considered knowledge of higher bureaucrats. *There were such enormous slopes.*

92

—But we drove up those slopes, the Road Administration Director observed quietly. Dammit, we were driving uphill the whole time.

—Well, it's always the same old shit, said Uncle Sune, but with a certain reflectiveness.

(The Yellow Book III:30)

Always the same old shit. While one attended elementary school, high school, the teacher's seminar, one was channeled step by step into a finer language. And into a more abstract one. One was only too willing to learn it. In high school one could tell the difference between children from lower-class homes and children from the middle-class homes. The children whose parents came from lower-class homes had a tougher, less illusion-prone language. I had the same experience when I became a teacher myself.

A view from the gutter from which all motivation for all actions became hard, egotistical, cynical.

The language of the middle class: the most insecure of all. It starts from the premise that in order to reach a higher level in the social hierarchy one has to act as if one had already arrived there. That creates a peculiar insecurity in the whole system. One knows the meaning of words, but not for sure.

For example, for several months now I've been "scared shitless." In another language one would call that fear of death. Fear of death gives the matter a completely different dimension, as if a higher intuition were present when one says "fear of death" instead of "scared shitless."

I don't see that this higher dimension exists.

Nothing has shown me as clearly as the experience of the last months that society has an unconscious. That may be attributed to the fact that fear has freed me from all the languages which I was once taught in order to protect myself. I am beginning to see with the terrible clarity of my boyhood period, with its anxious clarity.

The unconscious of society. The experimental animals, slowly tortured to death in laboratories, rubber tubes
94

inserted in their neck veins and stomachs, cancer cells planted in the livers of live dogs with long, thin syringes. The waiting rooms in the neurological clinics, the thin, trembling alcoholics at Storborn in Västerås.

All the time a terrible price is being paid. But to whom? And for what? What has been paid up to now for my existence?

. . .

Now so much snow has already melted away that the wet stones, the molded leaves of the previous year become visible everywhere.

I have always imagined paradise as being dry and hot, never moist.

In paradise there are no lies.

(The Blue Book III:5)

Four completely pain-free days. Uffe and Jonny were here again yesterday. I read them my horror story. They were not as impressed as I had imagined. They were of the opinion that it was a good beginning, but that there had to be a lot more action brought in. We discussed various continuations. Will the heroes make it to the tower on their own power and destroy the pain-causing ultrasound organ, or will they need some kind of help from outside?

Should they try to surround the tower? Should one man sacrifice himself in order to divert attention? Can one avoid these pain-causing sounds by plugging one's ears with wax?

Uffe has a bandage over his whole forehead. He had gotten an ice hockey puck on one eyebrow.

They had brought their magnifying glasses and sat a long time on my steps trying to set some shoelaces on fire. But the spring sun is much too weak still.

They entertain and distract me very much, these little fellows. They are so unproblematical somehow.

(The Yellow Book III:31)

Something is happening just now about which I hardly dare to speak, out of fear that mentioning it is going to make it untrue again.

The pains disappeared twelve days ago. Often I feel somewhat tired, somewhat dizzy, but that could just as easily be the normal spring fever. I have been to the store four times to do my shopping.

Then was it, after all, perhaps nothing so bad? A kidney stone? Kidney gravel that has been passed? These symptoms actually correspond very well to kidney stone symptoms.

Incidentally, kidney stone pains are considered to be among the severest possible. Stronger than labor pains, it says in an old issue of *Scientific American*.

I have decided to wait another week before I begin to hope.

(The Yellow Book III:32)

When I myself was small or still the same age: the strange, somewhat stuffy sweat smell of the gym way up under the roof, the pull-up bars around the walls, the feeling of wanting to do things for which one didn't have enough strength, of being a man and a boy at the same time. And that almost vegetative semisleep during the classes back then during prepuberty, the way one sat there playing strange games with one's own fingers, trying to interweave them in various ways, as if one were sitting in one's own brain weaving about in it: in order to understand its labyrinths.

I thought for a long time that this strange, sleepy condition had something to do with the monotony of school, but that's not true, I suppose.

Now I experience the same thing again: it is as if vitality had been slowed down, as if it were preparing for a big change.

In my case that is because I have the crisis of an illness behind me.

The peculiar, quiet melancholy of boyhood.

Apparently I'll have to live through this age anew.

(The Yellow Book III:33)

4. Interlude

(no notes whatsoever for thirty-three days)

April 6th. The pains are beginning to go away. Now only emptiness.

(The Damaged Notebook IX)

April 8th. All day long the barking of a dog could be heard, who must be new in this neighborhood. It comes from the south, terribly complaining and monotonous. Perhaps it is on a chain?

My problem: Although I don't have any pains anymore, something else is tormenting me instead; I'm beginning to hope and at the same time I don't dare to hope because they can recur at any time.

I think a great deal about one thing: since this letter which I burned, the District Hospital hasn't said a word. If it really had been cancer, logically they would have written again when they didn't hear from me; it is clear, after all, that they keep track of their patients. So it was a trifle, some inflammation. An inflammation of the diaphragm?

But what if they simply misfiled me?

I have begun to avoid the mailbox.

(The Yellow Book IV:1)

April 9th. Hope is almost as difficult as the other. But one is simply more used to hoping and fearing than to find oneself in the middle of what one had hoped or feared.

What I have learned: that there is no real escape from life.

One can only postpone the decision with cunning and cleverness. But there is no way out. It is a totally closed system, and at the exit there is only death. And that naturally is no exit at all.

I am a body. Nothing but a body. Everything which has to be done, which can be done, must happen within this body.

(The Yellow Book IV:2)

I've been thinking about Paradise, of all things. I also started to sand down the front door, it needs a new coat of paint, the old coat peeled off during the winter and hangs down in shreds. Surprisingly, I found three cans of paint in a kitchen cabinet, they must have been there since the early sixties, since I was married.

Paradise opens up interesting problems. What is an infinitely continuous state of happiness?

One thinks of an orgasm naturally. An orgasm, a big, wonderful orgasm, which suddenly surprises one by not stopping. It goes on minute after minute, hour after hour. It is so intense, so white hot, that one cannot think, but one feels that something tremendous is taking place, one begins to long for a tiny pause, only a fraction of a tenth of a second, to be able to reflect, but this tremendous pleasure simply continues, it continues hour after hour . . .

Paradise? I experienced all that recently.

Paradise must consist of the stopping of pain. That means, however, that we live in Paradise as long as we have no pain! And we don't even know it.

Happy and unhappy people live in the same world, and they don't even know it!

I have the feeling as if during the past months I have been walking around my own life in a fantastic, mysterious maze, and now I have returned precisely to that spot at which I began. But, since I moved outside the normal dimensions, right and left somehow got exchanged. My right hand is now my left one, my left hand my right one.

Returned into the same world and see it now as a happy one.

104

The shreds of peeled paint on the door belong to a mysterious work of art.

(The Yellow Book IV:3)

I should have used the time better than to fritter it away as an elementary school teacher at Väster Våla and now to raise bees here in voluntary early retirement.

Table of art forms according to their level of difficulty

1. Eroticism
2. Music
3. Poetry
4. Drama
5. Pyrotechnics
6. Philosophy
7. Surfing
8. The art of the novel
9. Glass painting
10. Tennis
11. Water colors
12. Oil painting
13. Rhetoric
14. The art of cooking
15. Architecture
16. Squash
17. Weight lifting
18. Politics
19. High trapeze
20. Parachute jumping
21. Mountain climbing
22. Sculpture
23. Bicycle acrobatics
24. Juggling
25. The art of aphorisms

26. Building fountains
27. Fencing
28. Artillery

One I cannot fit in: the art of bearing pain. That has to do with the fact that up to now no one has been able to make an art of it. We are therefore dealing with a unique art form whose level of difficulty is so high that no one exists who can practice it.

(The Blue Book IV:1)

A World Dominated by Truth

On Planet Number 3 in System 13 of Aldebaran there is a civilization which, without the use of symbolic connections, deals directly with reality.

The idea, for example, that a figure on a sheet of paper can represent something other than itself is completely foreign to the unusually strong, many-segmented centipedes which represent the highest level of civilization on the planet.

That they are strong is their good fortune. Since they know no other symbol for an object than the object itself, they have to drag a lot of things around with them. On this planet the expression "a powerful rhetoric" really has meaning.

If one wants to say, for example: "A stone warmed by the sun," there's only one possibility. One puts a stone warmed by the sun in the hand or better said, in the paw, of the person with whom one is speaking.

If you want to say "A huge stone on the peak of a mountaintop," there's only one possibility of expressing this sentence. Namely, that of dragging a huge stone to the top of a mountain.

Under these circumstances the creation of a lyrical poem becomes a test of strength which will continue to exist for generations in all of its heroic clarity.

Most of the sonnets created by this civilization look approximately like Stonehenge: gigantic, ceremonious rows of stones, which the heroes of prehistory, groaning and moaning, with bulging veins, erected according to an ancient design.

108

In this civilization lies are, of course, something totally impossible. If one wants to say "I love you," there's only one possibility, namely doing it. If one wants to say: "I don't love you," there is also only one possibility, and that consists of avoiding doing it. If one can.

In a world where the symbol invariably coincides with the object and, therefore, no object can ever be represented by ridiculous little sounds or a series of ludicrous little signs on a piece of paper, signs which, taken precisely, have nothing to do with other things, except in our fragile, haphazard social conventions. In such a world truth will coincide with sense, lies with nonsense.

In such a world the only substitution for a lie consists, naturally, in talking so confusedly, so nonsensically, that one cannot make oneself understood.

Normal conversation, chitchat, is conducted in the following manner on this planet. The inhabitants take a variety of tiny objects out of leather pouches they carry around: glass balls, little stones of various colors, prettily polished wooden sticks, and exchange them with each other.

The price of truth is high. Of all the highly developed civilizations in the region of the old central suns in the center of the Milky Way there is none which lives as isolated as this one.

Naturally one cannot think about astronomy. One doesn't talk about galaxies if one has to move them in order to name them. Even the concept "planet" is, naturally, totally inconceivable.

These beings live on a reddish plain surrounded by high mountains.

For this plain itself, which theoretically is the same as "the world," they, of course, have no concept.

(The Blue Book IV:4)

When the pains stopped fourteen days ago, that was a return for me into a kind of original paradise. But the precondition for this was the pain. It was a form of truth.

Just the opposite of Uncle Sune's "always the same old shit."

Now one could create something like values again.

(The Blue Book IV:8)

Everything went well. The relatives came on Tuesday, they had even more children with them than I had feared, took over the whole house, every spot, with sleeping bags, blankets, and provisional junk.

They were of the opinion that I looked a little pale, the women found the house a bit run-down, too many coffee cups with these impossible dry grounds. Nonetheless, it went well.

No one noticed anything unusual.

They stayed one day less than I had feared. Possibly I had a childish terror that the pains would begin again just because they were there.

Nothing else happened, however, other than I got a little tired.

I notice that I no longer like to be disturbed in my habits. On Wednesday, for example, the two little boys came by, got frightened about all the goings-on in the little house. I saw them disappear shyly behind the fence.

And I haven't even managed to write a new chapter for their horror story.

Naturally, I had imagined that this terrible organ, whose ultrasound produces pains, should be blown up in the next chapter; it would be revealed that this flute had very remarkable characteristics. It would be able to play away the whole spook.

Now I have to let the thing rest for a while. I hope they will come again. They are, so to speak, the only literary public I have.

I felt throughout a kind of curiosity about the reactions of the Manngårdhs, didn't dare, however, to ask as many questions as I actually had wished.

Do they see me as a completely normal relative, at

whose house one stays overnight instead of spending money for an expensive hotel on the way to Sälen, or do they consider it their duty *to look in on me*? It became clear to me that it has been a long time since I really gave a damn *what the world thought of me.*

I have not been able to discover anything really asocial about that besides the fact that I no longer demand the usual standard of living. I live without any income, which is very easy since I have no expenditures either.

Jan and I talked about old acquaintances. Our talk turned to Troäng. He knew him, after all, since he had been dealing with similar matters in the provincial government in Västerås. That whole scandal with the leukemia cases in northern Västmanland and with that special ecology commission.

Neither Manngårdh nor I had the slightest idea what he is doing now. A year ago there was some kind of rumor that he had joined the Brotherhood of the Holy Cross in Barkarö, but that kind of rumor arises inevitably in his circumstances. It is difficult for me to imagine him as a strict, ascetic member of an order. In contrast to me, who had actually always been a quite ascetic type, he was fairly sensual by nature.

One could see that in his school period, for example, in his relationship to girls.

What Manngårdh and I discussed was actually much more interesting. We talked about how this type of bureaucrat—naturally only if he is sensitive enough—sooner or later has to burn himself out, because he simply absorbs too many of the inner contradictions of society, he *internalizes them.*

That doesn't always have to take the extreme manifestation of Troäng who, in effect, vomited the entire conflict at the end of the affair when he was interviewed jointly with the Prime Minister on the evening television news.

One can sometimes detect it in the disquiet in their eyes. It ruptures as a stomach ulcer or expresses itself in a sudden exhaustion, in a divorce, but it does break through. One cannot live with too strong inner tensions, and these people internalize, after all, the aggregate conflict of society, attempting to live on both levels of communication.

After they went away, it became clear to me how interesting it is that Manngårdh of all people had brought up this matter. He is, after all, actually employed by the Employment Administration. Hopefully they were lucky in Sälen.

Troäng: something like that would never happen to me, since from the time I was an adult I have always had such a clear feeling of *standing apart*, of being basically asocial, even though I have always paid my taxes. Since the argument about the old age pensions I have not participated in any election.

Even my way of reacting to the illness is, naturally, asocial.

(The Yellow Book IV:12)

M. had a funny characteristic: she liked to lie about little things. Never any great deception; I was able to deceive her in significant matters for years if I really wanted to. She lied only about little things.

She might say that she had been shopping in Gamleby, while in actuality she had made her purchases in Fagersta. She might say that she spent a lonely evening weaving, while it was totally apparent that she had spent it weeding the strawberry patch.

I thought about that a lot until I came to the solution, which was really very simple:

With these little lies she created a realm of freedom.

Although this had no practical implications, it naturally made me somewhat insecure not to know in which store she had indeed been, and that gave her a small amount of control over me. Thus a realm developed in which she could make decisions without limitations.

That's naturally in no way an insinuation about her character, but it only shows that I—without knowing it—must have held her at a terrible distance.

Why is it that I don't want to have anything to do with people?

Because I don't want to give them any kind of *control* over me. But they have that anyway! Internal Revenue Service, Citizen's Registration Office, certainly. But much more the passions which are locked in my own body, because there already *the others* begin.

For example, the erotic disquiet (which is now gradually returning since the pains in the stomach are going away), this dull, indefinite hunger, this feeling of lacking

115

something, which, whether awake or asleep, pursues us in almost every moment of our lives.

What is it? The possibility of love in our bodies. The presence, the possible presence of another human being.

The humiliating, constant reminder that loneliness is not possible, that such a thing as a lonely human being cannot be.

That word "I" is the most meaningless word of the language. The dead point in the language.

(Just as a center always must be empty.)

(The Yellow Book IV:14)

I have decided not to call up M. It took me over two months to come to this decision, didn't it. I am really beginning to be a bit *slow*.

(The Yellow Book IV:21)

I am of the opinion that the soul is spherical (if indeed it has any form at all), a sphere, in which a faint light penetrates just a little ways below the rainbowlike shimmer of the surface, where sensations and reactions of consciousness whirl about like soap bubbles, constantly changing their color, but it's only a very little ways.

Deeper inside there are only feeble traces of light, approximately like those in very great ocean depths, and then darkness. Darkness, darkness.

But not a threatening dark. A motherly darkness.

(The Blue Book IV:9)

Recently I have repeatedly had a peculiar dream. It is about one of the beehives. I take off the cover and begin to brush off the frames in order to take out the hive. I am about to brush a bee off the edge of the frame when I discover that it looks odd somehow, shimmering blue, as it were. At first I don't grasp at all what is going on, then I look closer and notice that not one of the bees is a bee.

They are a totally different species. Some very intelligent, technically tremendously advanced beings from the farthest reaches of the universe, from a distant galaxy. They have simply taken over the beehive—heaven knows what has happened to the regular bees, but these beings appear to be used to living in cells similar to wax cells.

They converse with me without the slightest difficulty, and I simply don't quite understand how that is possible. They stem from a civilization of intelligent insects. Their entire planet has been destroyed by an exploding supernova, they have no spaceships, but fly their own bodies at the speed of light when they wish. In the earth's atmosphere they are not able to do that, however, because this would produce too great a buildup of heat.

Their brilliant glossy armor shines like knights' armor. What are they saying?

WE BEGIN AGAIN. WE NEVER GIVE UP.

(The Blue Book IV:10)

5. When God Awoke

About the way a small spider naps in the corner of the web it has built, God was napping for twenty million years in a distant nook of the universe.

That region was sparsely populated with galaxies. Nothing disturbed her sleep. She was hovering there like a giant jellyfish, thirteen parsecs in diameter, marvelous to look at with her continually changing pink, green, and deep blue color tones, which shimmered beneath the transparent surface of the umbrella.

To the entire endless universe, which stretched out for light-years in all directions about her, she lent a kind of freshness. Even though she was not palpable, a traveler still could have felt her presence, just as one feels it when approaching the coast from the interior on a sunny summer day, or when walking carefree through a fresh spring rain, letting the water run over one's face. She lent the empty space a unique feeling of freshness, of young green, yes, of being in love.

But during those twenty million years no traveler came into those distant regions, which were not only far beneath our optical horizon, but also lay far beneath our broadcast horizon.

For this wonderful and unique being, who was older than the universe and alien to time and space, who was both older and younger than all creation, larger than the entire universe and smaller than the tiniest elementary particle, twenty million years of sleep meant less than sleep. A moment of absence, just as when a motorist takes his eyes from the street for a moment in order to consider something.

123

When the highest being again turned her attention to the world, all perceptions were still the same. The deep, pulsing noise of periodic radio broadcasts in the next galaxy was the background for an endless multitude of more delicate sensations. The soft energy changes of the suns came and went like the wind in the leaves of an aspen woods, and like the dull pounding of waves on a wharf at night the gravitational collapses of dying supernovae reverberated from distant regions.

And as the highest of all frequencies, about like thousands of crickets and grasshoppers on a meadow, the thoughts from all inhabited worlds.

Among all these sounds there was one tone, a very distant, very faint one, which at first she did not even perceive. But in spite of all its faintness and minuteness this sound was so penetrating that it aroused her attention once she had noticed it. Just a moment earlier it had not been there. It was so plaintive that it sent a tremor through the gigantic body of something which, in human terms, could be characterized as motherly concern.

God had heard the prayers of human beings.

Three days passed before humanity noticed what was going on.

The first person to notice the change was a fifteen-year-old guerrilla soldier in a jungle area just south of Tanzania. He and his starving, dehydrated troop, with long, ulcerous scars on their legs, had just been discovered by a helicopter as they were trying to hide in the shade of a solitary cluster of trees in the middle of a steppe flooded with merciless noonday light.

124

The boy lay trembling next to an ammunition case, watching the helicopter approach. The muzzle fire of the machine guns was clearly visible already. In another moment he would die. He had been raised in a Christian mission. Seeing the helicopter approach and hearing how the dull, clattering noise of the rotor blades was drowned out by the harder clattering of the automatic weapons, he let a thought slip from himself:

God, destroy them!

The white flash, which turned the helicopter and its crew into a mass of strongly ionized particles driven away with the wind in a cloud, could be seen as far as the horizon.

The second helicopter, which was already approaching, crashed a few kilometers away with a shattering noise. The shaken crew groped about helplessly, blinded by the tremendous burst of light.

God, put an end to this, prayed a cancer patient in a hospital. The effect of the morphine was wearing off, and the glowing white pulsing pains in the lower right-hand part of his stomach, right above the loin, were returning, becoming stronger with every pulse.

At this moment the pain stopped and was replaced by something which seemed like a deafening silence. In his stomach area he felt only a faint pull, as if some hard object that had been pressing him there had been removed. He could breathe normally again. Five minutes later he attempted with immense care to pull up his leg.

After another five minutes he pressed the nurse's bell

125

like crazy. When the night nurse came through the door very belatedly he was standing in the middle of the room with a shy smile.

Give us, oh God, a lasting peace, the Archbishop of Åbo concluded his radio morning service. He said it in a deep seriousness and really meant every word he spoke.

Had he spoken this prayer but a tenth of a second earlier, he would have remained a common bishop, albeit an archbishop.

But since he spoke precisely at that special moment, he became a figure of world historical significance, yes truly the greatest figure of world history.

Three tenths of a second after the Archbishop of Åbo had said the word "peace," the control personnel in one of the huge subterranean rocket silos forming a chain in Outer Mongolia discovered that all of the ingenious instruments which control the condition of a rocket with multiple warheads—they can drop six hydrogen bombs simultaneously on six different cities—pointed to zero. This led to desperation, alarm, emergency measures. After six hours of hard work a team of specialists could conclude only that nothing could be saved. The eighty-meter-long rocket in its deep silo consisted from top to bottom of tremendously heavy, wonderfully glowing 24-carat gold. Soft, malleable, solid gold.

It took one more day for the world to discover that the same was true for all fissionable matter on earth and not only fissionable matter. Every weapon, every projectile back to iron-age swords in the museums had in the same instant been turned into gold.

126

At six p.m. the next day three members of the National Security Council of the United States, heavily sedated with psychopharmaceutical drugs, were transferred to a private psychiatric clinic. The remaining members observed their departure from a window on one of the upper floors of the Pentagon. They had the vacant gaze of people who don't want to see or hear anything more.

The first of the tremendous stock market crises, which within two days was to lead first to the dissolution of the money market and then to the dissolution of all finance, of every financial obligation, had already been rocking the stock markets of the world for ten hours.

The fall of the price of gold was, at first, enormous. Toward noon it had sunk to the price of a ton of coal in the year 1934.

The chaotic flight to the U.S. dollar, which started concurrently, had by one p.m. driven the price of the dollar to 12,340 ounces of gold. Within the next half-hour as a result of an unconfirmed rumor there was a panic run on Norwegian kroner, which within twenty-five minutes reached ten thousand times the value of the opening market.

In a special T.V. bulletin at two p.m., the president of the Norwegian National Bank announced in somber tones the news of national bankruptcy.

The television broadcast had only a very few viewers. For at this time, the citizens of Norway were engaged with private discoveries of such enormity that national bankruptcy left them totally indifferent.

For thousands of years the prayers of some people had

been very precise, very exact, whereas the prayers of others had been so vague and inexact that their wishes were articulated only in their dreams.

In northern Västmanland, between Ångelsberg and Ombenning, an old, retired lumberyard worker was sitting in his little house leafing randomly through the *Vestmanlands Läns Tidning* of the previous day. He was on the verge of dozing off. His eyes were blinking into the light, the flies were humming through the room.

A discreet knocking on the door gave him a start. When he opened his eyes, murmured a subdued "Come in!" and then saw six perfectly dressed waiters bringing in huge baskets of freshly cooked crabs in dill, caraway cheese as large as tractor wheels, carrying crates of ice-cold brandy, he accepted that with equanimity and concluded that he had, in fact, fallen asleep.

The first cymbal and the sound of the small flute gave him another start. The waiters had disappeared.

Arrayed in a shimmering blue transparent garment, the first of the five dancers began the dance. Her fantastically mobile navel circled under heavy jewelry hanging between her firm, small breasts. She smiled an infinitely inviting smile.

With firm steps the lumberyard worker went to the door and locked it. On the way back he noticed that the rheumatism in his left knee had disappeared without a trace.

At this point in time billions of people all over the world made the same discovery. The god who had so surprisingly begun to hear their prayers didn't seem to possess any kind of moral compunctions, not a trace of decency.

128

The power which was able to transform the giant projectiles laden with atomic weapons in one fell swoop into towers of gold soon showed itself just as willing to change the wrinkled wife of an elderly lieutenant colonel into a beautiful blond young man or to drown the nursery of the Social Welfare Department on Appelbergsgatan in Stockholm with a hurricane of Strauss waltzes and popping champagne corks.

The whole world was bustling with an apparently immeasurable army of eager servants, who would suddenly appear in order to provide every human being with everything he had secretly wished for. The thronging, the dancing, the public copulation in the streets of Europe was indescribable on that second day. Sporadic, vague radio reports from neighboring continents revealed that similar conditions had broken out there.

It was fascinating to watch the collapse of the church or, rather, of the churches. In the middle of the third day, approximately at the same time that His Majesty the King announced that all political parties had refused to assume the burden of government, approximately at the same time that Moscow and Washington announced that all official activities had ceased and the Communist Party of China announced the beginning—as scheduled —of the utopian phase, the missive from the Bishop's Conference, which had been anticipated for several days, was made public.

It was a masterwork of careful formulation. It began with the declaration that God's ways and the depth of nature were impenetrable and no one could dictate to the Almighty what means He should use.

Further it was hinted that there was also a demonic

power in the world, and a true Christian must always decide in his own conscience which prayers were in accordance with the will of God.

Even if this beginning of a new era in history were proof of God's goodness and omnipotence, the Bishop's Conference must not fail to point out the new temptations which this change, which certainly would not be perpetuated in all eternity, had, of necessity, to bring to every good Christian. In this period marked by tremendous upheaval, the Bishop's Conference saw itself compelled to admonish believers to be extremely circumspect in their prayers.

These words were spoken to the wind.

For the first time in its existence mankind had become familiar with a completely new kind of generosity, the boundless geniality, the indolent, yes completely nihilistic love of all creation which only that being can foster which has created it.

One can also express it this way:

Humankind, tormented for thousands of years by the strange and unhappy misconception of having a demanding and virtually inimical father figure above it, had recognized its error within a very few days.

Instead there was a mother.

As the human situation rapidly began to defy linguistic description and approached a realm for which there are no words, the DEATH OF LANGUAGE began.

One of the last speech fragments contained the message:

IF GOD LIVES, EVERYTHING IS ALLOWED.

(The Blue Book V:1)

6. Memoirs of Paradise

Birch wood. Swampland. The first sign that the trees are beginning to put out leaves. How terribly quickly winter has passed! I'm not sure whether I want the springtime yet at all. I am not yet ready for it. Loneliness grows in me like compost. The strangest plants shoot out of it. Doubt.

And every morning the same fear, that the pains will come again. The whole winter I had pains. Now I am suffering just as much from the fear of the pain. I observe myself very exactly: whether I have become weaker, whether walking is more of a strain for me, whether the trip to the grocer tires me more than before. I let the car sit, less to save gas than to put myself to the test. That means that I lose a whole morning, but I really don't know what I would have done with this time otherwise.

The human being, this strange creature, hovering between animal existence and hope.

I really don't know more than that about the meaning of the universe, no more than that about the purpose of it all: the molecules, the molecular chains, consciousness, sonnets and sestines, the underground rockets laden with atomic weapons, the frescoes of Michelangelo, the binominal theorem, and Monteverdi's madrigals, about the purpose of all of that, I don't know any more than any moss-covered old stone behind the beehives in the garden knows. Not any more than a mosquito knows. Than an amoeba in a stagnant puddle.

The history of humankind has not yet progressed very far. Actually it is still in its beginnings.

The fear of going mad is basically the fear of becoming another:

but we are doing that all the time.

What does not destroy me, makes me stronger. (Nietzsche)

Swampland. Birch trees. Coltsfoot blooms along the ditches. Most of the bee colonies have come back to life again. My friend Nicke, for example, who was run over by a truck when, on a day in September 1952, he wanted to ride his bike home during the breakfast break. I often think of him when I see something unusual, something which really interests me. Then I wonder what Nicke would have said about that. "Now I'm seeing that for you, Nicke." It is an enormously powerful experience. One *is* somehow identical with the people one has known.

The fifties. What do I remember about them? Little blue streetcars ran through Stockholm. Herbert Tingsten talked on T.V. The referendum about additional social security, which never interested me a great deal. The referendum about left- or right-hand traffic, which revealed that everybody wanted to keep left-hand traffic.

How were the girls dressed in the fifties? Didn't they wear cotton dresses which went way below their calves, and wide belts? Didn't they talk differently somehow? I don't remember precisely.

In the summer as little boys, yes even as high school students, we often sat on the locks of Färmansbo and fished. The lazy, tough, no not tough, but melancholy Kolbäcks River forms a little waterfall there. At this
134

point there was a small island with the remnants of an old ironworks. Earlier masses of umbrella mushrooms grew there.

On the southern end of the island is the Färmansbo lock. A path leads to it, which is shaded by such high trees that it is utterly transformed into a green tunnel. Ancient algae move on the stone banks of the canal.

At the lock itself the water is deep, coal black—the Kolbäcks River does not bear this name by accident—and at high water it creates black whirlpools, which always fascinated us when we were boys.

As early as May we would spend whole afternoons there, the pike were very active around that time. Several of us were living in summer houses our parents had in the neighborhood, others were the children of local residents.

Naturally, now and again it would happen that we got a fish on the hook, dramatic episodes with giant pike, who tore the golden glittering lure and disappeared with the whole thing in their mouths, great pike who continued to writhe in the grass like snakes, and sometimes one of us would slip on a wet stone and fall into the black, always cold water.

But I don't think that fishing was the most important thing about this lock.

The black, flowing water was kin to the black darkness in our own pupils.

We would sit there, look down, and talk about strange things with one another.

The bicycles lay in a heap behind some bushes, it was always difficult to get by the lockkeeper's house, because

135

the lockkeeper, an elderly man, didn't have much under-standing for a bunch of little boys running down to the lower locks. He was always afraid that they would fool around with the lock holes and change the water level, which was not very convenient for him, since it meant walking half a kilometer when one of the lock holes was opened which was supposed to be shut.

(By the way, bicycles played an enormous role for us then; they were on a par with domestic animals.)

Nicke was a very amusing boy. He had something of a squirrel in him. He was always wide awake. I had the impression that he simply saw more than the others. That he listened better than the others. He also was the one who discovered that one could hear the otters on the riverbank at sunset. An incredibly faint sound which none of us had noticed, although it had always been there.

A small, thin, tanned, incredibly wiry boy, who could climb the highest pines simply by pressing his knees against the bark and going up arm over arm. Once he swallowed a small live whitefish just to prove that one could do that.

He placed great value on proving that there were things which one could do although no one had consid-ered it possible. If he had lived in the fifteenth century and had not been run over by a truck, then in time he would certainly have discovered a new continent.

He was what I call a weather-sensitive person. He knew for hours in advance, when there wasn't a single cloud to be seen in the sky, that a storm was on the way. Storms did not make him restless, tired like other people.

I have the feeling they simply energized him, put him almost into a state of ecstasy.

When the hail beat down on the lock chamber until the whirlpools of the black water disappeared in a cloud of foam, until our fishing rods and the cans with the worms lay deserted, and we ourselves cowered breathless in a deserted blacksmith shop between old scrap iron, snakes, and nettles, one could see him dancing around outside in the downpour like a little dervish, often half naked, since he would get spankings from his mother when he came home with wet clothes.

I can still see him in front of me when I close my eyes, a wild little dervish dancing around ecstatically in a hailstorm on the rough-hewn stones from the eighteenth century glittering with rain, out there by the Färmansbo locks.

As if the rainstorm had been his father.

A little human being locked in its own secret.

I often ponder what he might have become. A sawmill worker like his father? The discoverer of the Mornington Islands? But then what is left to discover?

He always gave the impression that he was meant for something very special.

We were all meant for something different.

Contemplating the people I met in the course of my life: teachers, friends, girls, chance acquaintances, faithful old companions, relatives, it becomes clear to me that I did not know one of them, I say not a single one, not even my former wife and not my lover either.

One meets a new person, one whom one finds interesting. One attempts, as they say, to "place" him or

137

her. (I even try that with these ladies and gentlemen who read the news on television.)

One searches one's memory for faces which look like the one which one sees before him. The slow movements of the eyelids correspond with those of a speaker at the Biologists' Association, the corners of the mouth are the same as those of a chemistry lecturer in Uppsala in the fifties. In short: one picks a tone of voice here, a facial expression there.

One places the unknown with the aid of the known. The psychoanalyst in his analysis room (or whatever that's called; I've never been in one) does the same thing in principle: he brings together experiences and memories in order to discover the key to the new, unknown with which he is confronted.

But what we reconstruct this way, what we cast back for, jingling this bunch of keys to once-seen faces, doesn't unlock the unknown. We explain riddles with riddles.

But, after all, that is damn near the same thing as if one were to buy a second copy of *Länstidningen* in order to check a piece of news which one had not found credible in one's own copy of the newspaper.

Deep within, every human being hoards a pitch-black riddle. The darkness of the iris is nothing other than the starless night, the darkness deep in the eye is nothing other than the darkness of the universe.

Only as a riddle is a human being large and distinct enough. Only a mystical anthropology does him justice.

It was, of course, normal for Nicke to swim and dive like a fish. He dove down to the bottom of the deep lock chamber and released the trawl hooks which had been

138

caught there in the junk of three centuries. He held fast to old tree roots and wire cables, his hair floated around his head like sea grass, the lean body leveled horizontally in the stream; he looked like someone who was flying with tremendous speed, like an angel, whose normal reality is a state of suspension.

The water surface above him was a distant, glittering roof. The powerful water masses of the locks caused a constant soft creaking and groaning of the massive, tarred oak poles of the lock doors, which penetrated down to him like the ticking of a distant, giant clock. The voices of his playmates could not be heard anymore. He was absolutely without fear. The long water algae in the depths, where the stones went into the bottom, fluttered like the long hair of women.

He did not see the faces of the playmates, thin little ovals which bent worshipfully over the edge of the lock. He did not know how much time passed. Perhaps they would be gone when he came to the surface again, perhaps it would be a completely new era.

He was hovering. He was moving with great speed. He thought: I am holding on tightly. Carefully he loosened one hand, because he wanted to see whether the other arm was strong enough to hold him, but he felt that the current was too strong, it pulled him in the direction of the lock hole, which shimmered like a silver square opening far back in the deep green space in which he now found himself.

At this moment he discovered the lure for which he had dived. Or, better said, an object which could have been the lure.

It glittered like gold in the muddy basin approximately one meter beneath him.

And for a moment he imagined the long, undulating algae were the hair of the Kolbäck's daughters who were guarding this glittering treasure.

He grasped that there was only one way to get the lure without being driven helplessly by the current to the lock hole (and that was dangerous because one couldn't get through it, one would get stuck in it and drown), namely to swing his legs around slowly and try to grasp this glittering thing—whatever it might be—with the toes of his right foot.

As soon as he moved into the current, it seized him. Every time he attempted to reach this gold-glittering thing which had to be the lure, his toes stirred up little clouds of slime, which covered it completely. His lungs were hurting from the lack of oxygen.

We begin again. We never give up, he thought.

Above him was the whole summer. A soft wind was moving through the trees. On the other side of the island a kingfisher hovered above the water in the open part of the stream. From a distance the noise of an EPA-tractor could be heard, one of these cheap tractors, made from the front part of a truck and which, back in wartime, were used by farmers when they couldn't obtain any real tractors.

Swarms of doves were following the tractor in its course.

It was our landscape and yet it was not ours. It was our lives which had begun and yet they were not ours.

140

I have never been as wise as at that time. I knew how alien I was, but I also knew that the others were just as alien. In the universe no one is at home.

When Nicke came to the surface again, he was almost blue in the face from the lack of oxygen. Only with effort could he swim to the side, and after we had pulled him up over the stone embankment, it was almost five minutes before he could speak. He lay there and gasped for air like a small, very slimy fish. A scent of coarse basin slime, of ancient stones, of bleached seaweed and rotting muck surrounded him.

Gradually we grasped why he had swum so poorly when he came to the surface, and why he had had so much difficulty getting himself up the embankment. His right hand was a fist. He had kept his right hand locked tightly around some object.

We thought he would die. In the middle of this warm June day he was trembling from cold.

—What happened? we asked him.

At first his only answer was the chatter of his teeth. Finally, he tried to say something, and after a while he succeeded in speaking clearly enough for us to understand him.

—The lure wasn't there, he said. I didn't find it.

—But what have you got in your hand then?

He looked at it as if he were totally unaware that his hand was a balled fist.

—What have you got? What have you got?

We actually danced around him with excitement. It was clear to us that it couldn't be the lure because otherwise the hooks would have cut into his hand.

141

He opened it slowly, as if it had been cramped much too long. He seemed to be just as curious as we were about what would actually be there.

We were very still, breathless.

From the bottom of the Färmansbo lock Nicke had brought up a heavy gold coin, a gold ducat from the time of King Carl XIV Johan, the only one which has ever been found there.

(The Blue Book VI:1)

7. The Damaged Notebook

The gaze of Grandmother Tekla's eyes, this age-old look. The same darkness as that of the universe out there between the galaxies.

She was born in the Berg community in 1870, and she lived until last year. A small, waddling old lady in the Hallstahammar old age home, quite alert when one came to visit her, a pretty glass bowl with candies on the walnut dresser, a world of total security.

During the hundred years which she lived, she never had seen a reason, I believe, to wonder why she existed. Oh, to be sure, she had her religion, and that, of course, explained everything.

Have begun (even at the grocer's) to look people in the eye, as if their gaze had something special to say, I mean, as if one could read some kind of answer in it.

I have begun to harbor the peculiar notion they might perhaps see something which I don't see.

Yesterday a small lizard came to the back balcony and warmed itself in the April light.

It lay very still. I may be wrong, but I had the impression it actually changed its color to match the various silver-gray shades of the boards.

I lay on my stomach and looked at it a bit closer. That's when I discovered the tiny eye.

It had a blackness of a different kind, the wide-awake, sober blackness of reptiles.

Compared to the eye of a reptile, the eye of a mammal appears misty, half intoxicated with warm pulsations of life.

A reptile looks directly out into the darkness with a sober gaze.

Heaven knows what it sees. Something—different?

(The Blue Book VII:12 [the last entry])

. . . since three o'clock in the morning more and more intensely from the old spot, branching out down to the loins and to the diaphragm, at first with the usual degrees of severity, then up to the "white hot" level.

I knew that I had only been granted a pause.

Strangely I have the feeling that I have used it well.

(The Damaged Book II:1)

Ambulance 90000.
Central clinic 13 71 00 (switchboard).

(The Damaged Book II:2)

Throwing up everything with a kind of stubborn regularity. Even honey water. But it's all right in very little swallows. Slight fever.

Trip to the mailbox—like a polar expedition.

(The Damaged Book II:3)

Gave the dog to the Olssons on the Skrivar farm. Short, strange goodbye. He had gotten half a cheese as a parting gift, appeared somehow distracted and uninterested in spite of that. Dragged the cheese from one end of the room to the other. Was restless, yowled. Will be well taken care of.

(The Damaged Book II:4)

Good night, ladies. For three days it was gone, but now it is coming back again, in shorter and shorter intervals.

The unpleasant similarity between pain and lust. Both consume one's total attention, one sees nothing else anymore. It is like a woman one loves. News, the weather, changes in nature, it even manages to extinguish fear. It is a realm in which truth dominates irrevocably.

People now look in a bit more frequently, they say very openly that I should go to the hospital. They are practical, the people in northern Västmanland. One never says in Västmanland: "He has died." One says: "He is gone dead." They are afraid that I "will go dead."

Cannot read the newspaper anymore. I read, that is, I let my gaze wander from word to word, but every word contains nothing but pain. Even worse is the feeling that it doesn't have anything to do with me. Lately they have been talking about something they call the "Information Bureau."* Their problems are not my problems anymore. I would like to know what this "Information Bureau" is. I imagine a bureau which can answer all questions.

Why me of all people?

Why am I of all people mortal?

Why do I of all people have this pain?

Why am I of all people identical with this pain?

Why am I of all people identical with someone who experiences this pain?

Why?

(The Damaged Book II:5)

*"Information Bureau": the Swedish Secret Service (translator's note).

The problem with these women: they recognized that I wanted much too little. Women are ready for anything when they recognize that one wants it.

I have wanted much too little. My whole life long. People never had the feeling that I had any *need* of them. The last three months have made me *real*. That is terrible.

(The Damaged Book III:1)

Threw up the whole night long. The last April. Discoloration of the skin on the forearms. Large brown spots.

Today it became clear to me that the whole idea of suicide is absurd.

There is absolutely no way out. We are immersed *totally and completely* in reality, in history, in our own biology. The possibility of imagining one's own death amounts to a linguistic misconception. Similar to the possibility of calling oneself "you." Or like the possibility of calling oneself by a name.

The blackness of the pupil is identical with the blackness between the galaxies.

(The Damaged Book III:2)

1–8:	cleaned, the queens in good condition.
9–11:	frozen, not cleaned.
12–14:	in good condition, the queens possibly too old, the frames have to be attended to, new combs.
15–16:	standing empty since fall 1971. Not attended to.

(The Damaged Book IV:1)

Spring, early summer winds, the scent of lilacs. The pounding of short, restless waves on the beach, the swarm of whitefish. The yellowed little stems of the dried reed.

A swarm of whitefish stands very still, as if it were one single body. How can a single whitefish know that the others are standing just as still?

Then a shadow falls there, the shadow of somebody who is bending over the water, and the swarm scatters in an explosion of lightning-quick reflexes, every one in a different direction, just as quickly as the light reflects in the water above them.

Nothing is left to reveal that they were there.

After they are gone, it's hard to believe that they just were there.

(The Damaged Book V:1)

What's happening to me now is disgusting, horrible, and degrading, and nobody will bring me to accept it or to persuade myself that it is somehow good for me.

It is disgusting to be at the mercy of an idiotic blind pain, fits of vomiting, and this entire secret inner dissolution, which is stupid and offensive, no matter what kind of an explanation there may be for it.

The usual heresy consists in denying the existence of a god who has created us. It is a much more interesting heresy to imagine that possibly a god has created us and then to say that there isn't the least reason for us to be impressed by that fact. And certainly not to be thankful for it.

If there is a god it is our duty to say no.

If there is a god then it is the task of the human being to be his negation.

We begin again. We never give up.

My duty in these days, weeks or, at the worst, months which are still left, consists in saying a great, clear NO.

(The Damaged Book VI:1–3)

I, I, I, I, . . . after only four times already a senseless word.

(The Damaged Book VI:4)

Although it is the second week in May, it's snowing today in all of Västmanland. The ambulance is coming to get me at four o'clock. I hope that the streets will not be too slippery.

One can always hope that there won't be an accident. One can still hope.

(The Damaged Book VII:0)

Afterword

Lars Gustafsson is an engaging personality. He has the capacity for including his audience in his thinking and creating a sense of give and take, an exchange of ideas, enthusiasms, and perceptions. If Guntram Weber and I had not met Lars, attended his classes, watched him revel in his idiosyncratic standards of excellence, witnessed his undaunted capacity for doing, been struck by his "otherness," his seeming bravado, his almost rude self-confidence, we probably never would have undertaken to find and read his novels—works inaccessible to English-speaking readers. But knowing him, we were drawn to his writing. We asked ourselves, "Is this captivation glitter, an illusion, a clever deception, or is there substance?" What are the dynamics of Lars Gustafsson's *joie de vivre*? Would it be as contagious in his writing as in the flesh?

The last question must be answered by the individual reader. The questions of deception and dynamics, however, are dealt with in depth in the novel *The Death of a Beekeeper* as elsewhere in Lars Gustafsson's work. They are at the heart of his philosophy, his poetry, and his prose. For Lars Gustafsson consciously extends his philosophical convictions into his life and his creativity, believing that the precondition for freedom is our individual capacity to define ourselves. "More and more people," he says, "are realizing that the meaning or sense of their lives is the one they have to give to themselves."* But this self-definition functions as a mirror or a wall which redirects one's reality construct back toward oneself. Only in confronting a barrier does an image of self become precise. Lars sees this defining barrier as one's "limits." "The limits are the points where you discover reality, where you meet resistance. You say to yourself, 'I cannot go further in this direction; here I am ignorant.' A religious leader might say, 'Here my convictions stop.'"

*All author comments are drawn from two taped interviews conducted by Janet Swaffar with Lars Gustafsson on February 6 and April 25, 1979.

Modern man, says Lars Gustafsson, has succeeded in demonstrating to himself that there is no absolute certainty anywhere in his universe, be it in theology, philosophy, or even physics and mathematics. Rather than viewing uncertainty as cause for despair, Lars affirms the denial of absolutes as an opportunity for self-discovery. By discovering what you are not, you discover what you are. "God," says Lars, "comes into Descartes' philosophy only as a sort of geometrical question. That is to say, Descartes asks, 'What would be the case if God is systematically deceiving us; what would remain of solid truth?' He answers this question by saying that the one thing that remains solid, remains certain, is the fact that we doubt: *Cogito ergo sum*."

Doubting reality, then, becomes an exercise, a creation of reality. It is in this sense that Lars Gustafsson proposes that writing be an overt act of deception or, as he expresses it: "Writers have to pose to themselves the question, 'Are we counterfeiters?' When I speak about counterfeit, I mean giving value to things that are valueless, giving context to things which have no context. This is exactly the way to make literature."

Such a counterfeit reality is the raw material for the series of five novels of which *Beekeeper* is the last. All of the novels deal with a possible Lars Gustafsson, one of them even entitled *Mr. Gustafsson, Himself.** The author explains the process: "I took one personality, mainly my own childhood, my own youth up to the age of eighteen and then varied it into five different lives, strengthening one property of my personality here, weakening it in another by giving myself a little more of a certain talent, subtracting a talent there. That resulted in alternative lives, what I call the cracks in the wall. These five novels are an experiment with the possible lives of a certain organism. They are a set of premises."

Mr. Gustafsson, Himself (1971), *Woe* (1973), *The Family Reunion* (1975), *Sigismund* (1977), *The Death of a Beekeeper* (1979).

160

By experimenting with such a set of premises, Lars is seeking to create the unique rather than the representative. Delineating the unique in *The Death of a Beekeeper* involved a precision which, to its author, is comparable to viewing a subject through increasingly stronger lenses of a microscope. His micro-lenses are a series of superficially redundant notebooks, each serving a different objective, each possessing a different optical power, presenting the reader with stylistic variations of the same theme. Not Doris Lessing, Lars maintains, but his own working notebooks motivated the decision to use this narrative ploy. "As I came into my office [in Austin], I saw my own notebooks lying on the table. You know, the yellow notebook for my lectures and the blue notebook containing sketches for one book and a red notebook containing sketches for a third book, and it occurred to me that they all had their own language, their own style of writing."

The beekeeper's notebooks also function as variant inventories of the protagonist's life. The Blue Notebook purports to inventory his imagination. The Yellow Notebook contains an admixture of notations about household finances and personal comments about such events as the arrival of the diagnostic results from the District Hospital, the letter assumed to contain the news that the beekeeper has terminal cancer. This juxtaposition of economic pressures and death is not accidental, because Lars wants to imply that the lifeless exteriority of household finances contains death. The narrative fiction is that the Yellow Notebook is not reproduced except in terms of a "few indicative samples."

In contrast with the discursive Yellow and Blue notebooks, the Damaged Notebook conveys the tension and imminence of a memo pad and is ostensibly reproduced in full. It consists of local telephone numbers, terse observations, and notes about the course of the beekeeper's disease. It most clearly reflects the protagonist's physical state, demonstrating in its fragments the beekeeper's need to break off, his inability to finish. The terse notations register and catalogue intense experiences of pain and perception and, in so doing, locate and diffuse their otherwise overwhelming impact.

All the notebooks concentrate the focus of *Beekeeper* on a man who is discovering life in the process of dying. Yet it is not a book about dying. "People talk so much about fearing death," says Lars, "but very often they mean pain. If you ask the first person you meet what he is fearing, he will answer 'death,' but he will obviously mean pain. Death is something so tremendously empty and abstract."

Death is the remote limit in the beekeeper's life. More palpable by far in these pages is the experience of pain, portrayed with a particular poignancy: for it is through pain that the protagonist, an unabashedly egocentric man, meets his limits and thereby extends the meaning of his life.

This extension process is not morbid. From the outset the hero, nicknamed Weasel, is never unattractive, despite his self-centeredness. He has humor—"Proletarians of pain, unite!" he thinks in a doctor's waiting room—and imagination. All the notebooks testify to his capacity to engage the reader: even his capacity for rationalizing his behavior becomes a charming foible. The reader comes to admire the Weasel's facility for fabricating idiosyncratic conclusions, for reminiscing about a girl he cannot remember or about an argument whose substance is forgotten.

Gradually, however, the pain of the cancer refocuses his attention as it alternates with respites from pain. His perception of nature and of people changes. When he dreams of his bees, which he has viewed as a mindless collective organism, they are transformed into a totally different, highly differentiated species—as some very intelligent, technically "advanced beings from the farthest reaches of the universe." He views past events for the first time with something other than complete self-satisfaction, or at least with the dislocation essential to begin a reassessment of the potentials within himself: "Perhaps I should have used the time better."

162

He begins to reflect about the fact that he has never wanted to have anything to do with people before because he does not want to give them control. He concludes that this was a vain aspiration, since he finds one can deny others but not the innate human desire for intellectual and physical companionship. He is struck by the fact that: "That word 'I' is the most meaningless word in the language. The dead point in the language. Just as the center must always be empty." And what he learns is, "there is no real escape from life."

His pain has created an absolute other within his own body. He denies his pain much as Descartes denied God—as an affirmation of self. With this opposition of pain he has the means to discover a nascent self and escape the vacuum of his own egocentrism.

The Death of a Beekeeper, then, is a novel with a philosophical program, an undertaking which, in the popular mind, could easily cast it in the role of a dubious entertainment. And for this reason no one is more surprised and suspicious than Lars Gustafsson about the novel's popular success in Sweden and in Germany. He finds popularity a trifle suspect, maintaining that there is a "well-known media distinction between effect on the surface and affect which goes under the surface and becomes a profound effect. I mean, you can titillate millions of people for a few minutes and you can affect a few people to such an extent that they won't forget your ideas the rest of their lives. In the long run, the deep, profound impression can lead to literature's affecting many more people than a popular novel does."

In an era in which titillation and mass manipulation dominate the media marketplace, Lars Gustafsson's *The Death of a Beekeeper* may prove an anomaly: a book which epitomizes a profound individualism.

Janet King Swaffar

A Note on the Author

Lars Gustafsson was born on May 17, 1936, in Västerås, Sweden. He earned the equivalent of an American doctorate at the University of Uppsala in 1962, and his dissertation, *Language and Lies,* on Friedrich Nietzsche, Fritz Mauthner, and the American philosopher Alexander Bryan Johnson (under whom the author studied), has been published in several languages.

Through his writings on mathematics, sociology, history, philosophy, and literature, Gustafsson's influence has been strong in all quarters of the European academic community, but his essays and comments, notably the collection on *Utopia* (1969), have reached an even broader audience. He has published in virtually every area of *belles lettres*: novels, stories, poems, drama, literary criticism, and journalism, and from 1962 to 1972, he was the editor of *Bonniers Litterära Magasin,* the leading literary periodical of Sweden.

He is best known in his native land and, through an excellent translation, in Germany as well, for his related series of novels, *Mr. Gustafsson, Himself* (1971), *Woe* (1973), *Family Reunion* (1975), *Sigismund* (1977), and *The Death of a Beekeeper* (1979). Although each of these can be enjoyed alone, they are five variations on a common theme: "We begin again. We never give up."

Some New Directions Paperbooks

Walter Abish, *Alphabetical Africa*. NDP375.
  In the Future Perfect. NDP440.
  Minds Meet. NDP387.
Illangô Adigal, *Shilappadikaram*. NDP162.
Alain, *The Gods*. NDP382
Wayne Andrews. *Voltaire*. NDP519.
David Antin, *Talking at the Boundaries*. NDP388.
G. Apollinaire, *Selected Writings.*† NDP310.
Djuna Barnes, *Nightwood*. NDP98.
Charles Baudelaire, *Flowers of Evil.*† NDP71,
  Paris Spleen. NDP294.
Martin Bax, *The Hospital Ship*. NDP402.
Gottfried Benn, *Primal Vision.*† NDP322.
Wolfgang Borchert, *The Man Outside*. NDP319.
Jorge Luis Borges, *Labyrinths*. NDP186.
Jean-Francois Bory, *Once Again* NDP256.
E. Brock, *Here. Now. Always*. NDP429.
  The Portraits & The Poses. NDP360.
  The River and the Train. NDP478.
Buddha, *The Dhammapada*. NDP188.
Frederick Busch, *Domestic Particulars*. NDP413.
  Manual Labor. NDP376.
Ernesto Cardenal, *Apocalypse*. NDP441. *In Cuba*.
  NDP377. *Zero Hour*. NDP502.
Hayden Carruth, *For You*. NDP298.
  From Snow and Rock, from Chaos. NDP349.
Louis-Ferdinand Céline,
  Death on the Installment Plan NDP330.
  Journey to the End of the Night. NDP84.
Jean Cocteau, *The Holy Terrors*. NDP212.
  The Infernal Machine. NDP235.
M. Cohen, *Monday Rhetoric*. NDP352.
Robert Coles, *Irony in the Mind's Life*. NDP459.
Cid Corman, *Livingdying*. NDP289.
  Sun Rock Man. NDP318.
Gregory Corso, *Elegiac Feelings*. NDP299.
  Happy Birthday of Death. NDP86.
  Long Live Man. NDP127.
Robert Creeley, *Hello*. NDP451.
  Later. NDP488.
Edward Dahlberg, *Reader*. NDP246.
  Because I Was Flesh. NDP227.
Osamu Dazai, *The Setting Sun*. NDP258.
  No Longer Human. NDP357.
Coleman Dowell, *Mrs. October . . .* NDP368.
  Too Much Flesh and Jabez. NDP447.
Robert Duncan, *Bending the Bow*. NDP255.
  The Opening of the Field. NDP356.
  Roots and Branches. NDP275.
Dutch "Fiftiers," *Living Space*. NDP493.
Richard Eberhart, *Selected Poems*. NDP198.
E. F. Edinger, *Melville's Moby-Dick*. NDP460.
Russell Edson, *The Falling Sickness*. NDP389.
Wm. Empson, *7 Types of Ambiguity*. NDP204.
  Some Versions of Pastoral. NDP92.
Wm. Everson, *Man-Fate*, NDP369.
  The Residual Years. NDP263.
Lawrence Ferlinghetti, *Her*. NDP88.
  A Coney Island of the Mind. NDP74.
  Endless Life. NDP516.
  The Mexican Night. NDP300.
  The Secret Meaning of Things. NDP268.
  Starting from San Francisco. NDP220.
  Tyrannus Nix?. NDP288.
  Unfair Arguments . . . NDP143
  Who Are We Now? NDP425.
Ronald Firbank, *Five Novels*. NDP518.
F. Scott Fitzgerald, *The Crack-up*. NDP54.
Robert Fitzgerald, *Spring Shade*. NDP311.
Gustave Flaubert, *Dictionary*. NDP230.
Gandhi, *Gandhi on Non-Violence*. NDP197.
Goethe, *Faust*, Part I. NDP70.
Henry Green. *Back*. NDP517.
Allen Grossman, *The Woman on the Bridge*
  Over the Chicago River. NDP473.
John Hawkes, *The Beetle Leg*. NDP239.
  The Blood Oranges. NDP338.
  The Cannibal. NDP123.
  Death Sleep & The Traveler. NDP393.
  The Innocent Party. NDP238.
  The Lime Twig. NDP95.
  The Owl. NDP443.

Second Skin. NDP146.
Travesty. NDP430.
A. Hayes, *A Wreath of Christmas Poems*.
  NDP347.
Samuel Hazo. *To Paris*. NDP512.
H. D., *End to Torment*. NDP476.
  Helen in Egypt. NDP380.
  Hermetic Definition. NDP343.
  Trilogy. NDP362.
Robert E. Helbling, *Heinrich von Kleist*, NDP390.
Hermann Hesse, *Siddhartha*. NDP65.
C. Isherwood, *All the Conspirators*. NDP480.
  The Berlin Stories. NDP134.
Philippe Jaccottet, *Seedtime*. NDP428.
Alfred Jarry, *The Supermale*. NDP426.
  Ubu Roi. NDP105.
Robinson Jeffers, *Cawdor and Media*. NDP293.
James Joyce, *Stephen Hero*. NDP133.
  James Joyce/Finnegans Wake. NDP331.
Franz Kafka, *Amerika*. NDP117.
Bob Kaufman,
  The Ancient Rain. NDP514.
  Solitudes Crowded with Loneliness. NDP199.
Hugh Kenner, *Wyndham Lewis*. NDP167.
Kenyon Critics, *G. M. Hopkins*. NDP355.
H. von Kleist, *Prince Friedrich of Homburg*.
  NDP462.
Elaine Kraf, *The Princess of 72nd St*. NDP494.
P. Lal, *Great Sanskrit Plays*. NDP142.
Lautréamont, *Maldoror*. NDP207.
Irving Layton, *Selected Poems*. NDP431.
Denise Levertov, *Collected Earlier*. NDP475.
  Footprints. NDP344.
  The Freeing of the Dust. NDP401.
  The Jacob's Ladder. NDP112.
  Life in the Forest. NDP461.
  The Poet in the World. NDP363.
  Relearning the Alphabet. NDP290.
  The Sorrow Dance. NDP222.
  To Stay Alive. NDP325.
Harry Levin, *James Joyce*. NDP87.
Li Ch'ing-chao, *Complete Poems*. NDP492.
Enrique Lihn, *The Dark Room.*† NDP452.
García Lorca, *The Cricket Sings.*† NDP506.
  Deep Song. NDP503.
  Five Plays. NDP232.
  Selected Poems.† NDP114.
  Three Tragedies. NDP52.
Michael McClure, *Gorf*. NDP416.
  Antechamber. NDP455.
  Jaguar Skies. NDP400.
  Josephine: The Mouse Singer. NDP496.
Carson McCullers, *The Member of the*
  Wedding. (Playscript) NDP153.
Thomas Merton, *Asian Journal*. NDP394.
  Collected Poems. NDP504.
  Gandhi on Non-Violence. NDP197.
  News Seeds of Contemplation. NDP337.
  Raids on the Unspeakable. NDP213.
  Selected Poems. NDP85.
  The Way of Chuang Tzu. NDP276.
  The Wisdom of the Desert. NDP295.
  Zen and the Birds of Appetite. NDP261.
Henry Miller, *The Air-Conditioned Nightmare*.
  NDP302.
  Big Sur & The Oranges. NDP161.
  The Books in My Life. NDP280.
  The Colossus of Maroussi. NDP75.
  The Cosmological Eye. NDP109.
  Henry Miller on Writing. NDP151.
  The Henry Miller Reader. NDP269.
  Just Wild About Harry. NDP479.
  The Smile at the Foot of the Ladder. NDP386.
  Stand Still Like the Hummingbird. NDP236.
  The Time of the Assassins. NDP115.
Y. Mishima, *Confessions of a Mask*. NDP253.
  Death in Midsummer. NDP215.
Eugenio Montale, *It Depends.*† NDP507.
  New Poems. NDP410.
  Selected Poems.† NDP193.
Vladimir Nabokov, *Nikolai Gogol*. NDP78.
  Laughter in the Dark. NDP470.
  The Real Life of Sebastian Knight. NDP432.
P. Neruda, *The Captain's Verses.*† NDP345.
  Residence on Earth.† NDP340.

New Directions in Prose & Poetry (Anthology).
Available from #17 forward. #42, Fall 1981.
Robert Nichols, *Arrival.* NDP437.
Exile. NDP485. *Garh City.* NDP450.
Harditts in Sawna. NDP470.
Charles Olson. *Selected Writings.* NDP231.
Toby Olson, *The Life of Jesus.* NDP417.
George Oppen, *Collected Poems.* NDP418.
Wilfred Owen, *Collected Peoms.* NDP210.
Nicanor Parra, *Emergency Poems.*† NDP333.
Poems and Antipoems.† NDP242.
Boris Pasternak, *Safe Conduct.* NDP77.
Kenneth Patchen. *Aflame and Afun.* NDP292.
Because It Is. NDP83.
But Even So. NDP265.
Collected Poems. NDP284.
Doubleheader. NDP211.
Hallelujah Anyway. NDP219.
In Quest of Candlelighters. NDP334.
Memoirs of a Shy Pornographer. NDP205.
Selected Poems. NDP160.
Octavio Paz, *Configurations.*† NDP303.
A Draft of Shadows.† NDP489.
Eagle or Sun?† NDP422.
Early Poems.† NDP354.
Plays for a New Theater. (Anth.) NDP216.
J. A. Porter, *Eelgrass.* NDP438.
Ezra Pound, *ABC of Reading.* NDP89.
Classic Noh Theatre of Japan. NDP79.
Confucius. NDP285.
Confucius to Cummings. (Anth.) NDP126.
Gaudier Brzeska. NDP372.
Guide to Kulchur. NDP257.
Literary Essays. NDP250.
Love Poems of Ancient Egypt. NDP178.
Pound/Joyce. NDP296.
Selected Cantos. NDP304.
Selected Letters 1907-1941. NDP317.
Selected Poems. NDP66.
The Spirit of Romance. NDP266.
Translations.† (Enlarged Edition) NDP145.
James Purdy, *Children Is All.* NDP327.
Raymond Queneau, *The Bark Tree.* NDP314.
Exercises in Style. NDP513.
The Sunday of Life. NDP433.
We Always Treat Women Too Well. NDP515.
Mary de Rachewiltz, *Ezra Pound.* NDP405.
M. Randall, *Part of the Solution.* NDP350.
John Crowe Ransom, *Beating the Bushes.*
NDP324.
Raja Rao, *Kanthapura.* NDP224.
Herbert Read, *The Green Child.* NDP208.
P. Reverdy, *Selected Poems.*† NDP346.
Kenneth Rexroth, *Collected Longer Poems.*
NDP309.
Collected Shorter Poems. NDP243.
The Morning Star. NDP490.
New Poems. NDP383.
100 More Poems from the Chinese. NDP308.
100 More Poems from the Japanese. NDP420.
100 Poems from the Chinese. NDP192.
100 Poems from the Japanese.† NDP147.
Rainer Maria Rilke, *Poems from*
The Book of Hours. NDP408.
Possibility of Being. (Poems). NDP436.
Where Silence Reigns. (Prose). NDP464.
Arthur Rimbaud, *Illuminations.*† NDP56.
Season in Hell & Drunken Boat.† NDP97.
Edouard Roditi, *Delights of Turkey.* NDP445.
Selden Rodman, *Tongues of Fallen Angels.*
NDP373.
Jerome Rothenberg, *Poland/1931.* NDP379.
Pre-Faces. NDP511.
Seneca Journal. NDP448.
Vienna Blood. NDP498.
Saigyo,† *Mirror for the Moon.* NDP465.
Saikaku Ihara. *The Life of an Amorous*
Woman. NDP270.
St. John of the Cross, *Poems.*† NDP341.
Jean-Paul Sartre, *Baudelaire.* NDP233.

Nausea. NDP82.
The Wall (Intimacy). NDP272.
Delmore Schwartz, *Selected Poems.* NDP241.
In Dreams Begin Responsibilities. NDP454.
Kazuko Shiraishi, *Seasons of Sacred Lust.*
NDP453.
Stevie Smith, *Selected Poems,* NDP159.
Gary Snyder, *The Back Country.* NDP249.
Earth House Hold. NDP267.
Myths and Texts. NDP457.
The Real Work. NDP499.
Regarding Wave. NDP306.
Turtle Island. NDP381.
Enid Starkie, *Rimbaud.* NDP254.
Robert Steiner, *Bathers.* NDP495.
Stendhal, *The Telegraph.* NDP108.
Jules Supervielle, *Selected Writings.*† NDP209.
W. Sutton, *American Free Verse.* NDP351.
Nathaniel Tarn, *Lyrics . . . Bride of God.* NDP391.
Dylan Thomas, *Adventures in the Skin Trade.*
NDP183.
A Child's Christmas in Wales. NDP181.
Collected Poems 1934-1952. NDP316.
The Doctor and the Devils. NDP297.
Portrait of the Artist as a Young Dog.
NDP51.
Quite Early One Morning. NDP90.
Under Milk Wood. NDP73.
Lionel Trilling. *E. M. Forster.* NDP189.
Martin Turnell. *Art of French Fiction.* NDP251.
Baudelaire. NDP336.
Rise of the French Novel. NDP474.
Paul Valéry, *Selected Writings.*† NDP184.
P. Van Ostaijen, *Feasts of Fear & Agony.*
NDP411.
Elio Vittorini, *A Vittorini Omnibus.* NDP366.
Women of Messina. NDP365.
Vernon Watkins, *Selected Poems.* NDP221.
Nathanael West, *Miss Lonelyhearts &*
Day of the Locust. NDP125.
J. Williams, *An Ear in Bartram's Tree.* NDP335.
Tennessee Williams, *Camino Real.* NDP301.
Cat on a Hot Tin Roof. NDP398.
Dragon Country. NDP287.
The Glass Menagerie. NDP218.
Hard Candy. NDP225.
In the Winter of Cities. NDP154.
A Lovely Sunday for Creve Coeur. NDP497.
One Arm & Other Stories. NDP237.
A Streetcar Named Desire. NDP501.
Sweet Bird of Youth. NDP409.
Twenty-Seven Wagons Full of Cotton. NDP217.
Two-Character Play. NDP483.
Vieux Carré. NDP482.
Where I Live. NDP468.
William Carlos Williams.
The Autobiography. NDP223.
The Build-up. NDP223.
The Farmers' Daughters. NDP106.
I Wanted to Write a Poem. NDP469.
Imaginations. NDP329.
In the American Grain. NDP53.
In the Money. NDP240.
Many Loves. NDP191.
Paterson. Complete. NDP152.
Pictures form Brueghel. NDP118.
The Selected Essays. NDP273.
Selected Poems. NDP131.
A Voyage to Pagany. NDP307.
White Mule. NDP226.
W. C. Williams Reader. NDP282.
Yvor Winters, *E. A. Robinson.* NDP326.
Wisdom Books: *Ancient Egyptians,* NDP467.
Early Buddhists, NDP444; *English Mystics,*
NDP466; *Forest* (Hindu), NDP414; *Jewish*
Mystics, Francis, NDP423; *Spanish Mystics,* NDP442;
St. Francis, NDP477; *Sufi,* NDP424; *Taoists,*
NDP509; *Wisdom of the Desert,* NDP295; *Zen*
Masters, NDP415.

For complete listing request complete catalog from
New Directions, 80 Eighth Avenue, New York 10011   † Bilingual